KU-428-514

Liquidation

ALSO BY

Imre Kertész

Fiction

Fatelessness

Imre Kertész

Liquidation

TRANSLATED
FROM THE HUNGARIAN
BY
Tim Wilkinson

Harvill *Secker*
LONDON

Published by Harvill Secker, 2006

2 4 6 8 10 9 7 5 3 1

First published with the title *Felszámolás*
by Magvető Könyvkiadó, Budapest

First published in Great Britain in 2006 by
HARVILL SECKER
Random House
20 Vauxhall Bridge Road
London SW1V 2SA

Random House Australia (Pty) Limited
20 Alfred Street, Milsons Point, Sydney,
New South Wales 2061, Australia

Random House New Zealand Limited
18 Poland Road, Glenfield,
Auckland 10, New Zealand

Random House South Africa (Pty) Limited
Isle of Houghton, Corner of Boundary Road & Carse O'Gowrie,
Houghton 2198, South Africa

The Random House Group Limited Reg. No. 954009
www.randomhouse.co.uk/harvillsecker

A CIP catalogue record for this book is available from the British Library

ISBN 9781843432357 (from January 2007)
ISBN 1843432358

Papers used by Random House are natural, recyclable products made from wood grown in sustainable forests; the manufacturing processes conform to the environmental regulations of the country of origin

Printed and bound in Germany by GGP Media GmbH, Pößneck

For Magda

Then I went back into the house and wrote, It is midnight. The rain is beating on the windows. It was not midnight. It was not raining.

—Beckett, *Molloy*

Liquidation

Let us call our man, the hero of this story, Kingbitter. We imagine a man, and a name to go with him. Or conversely, let us imagine the name, and the man to go with it. Though this may all be avoided anyway since our man, the hero of this story, really is called Kingbitter.

Even his father was already called that.

His grandfather too.

Kingbitter was accordingly registered on his birth certificate under the name Kingbitter: that, therefore, is the reality, on which—reality, that is to say—Kingbitter did not set too much store nowadays. Nowadays—a late year of the passing millennium, in the early spring of, let us say, 1999, on a sunny morning at that—reality had become a problematic concept for Kingbitter, but, more serious still, a problematic *state.* A state from which, on the report of Kingbitter's most private feelings, it was reality above all that was lacking. If he were in some way compelled to make use of the word, Kingbitter invariably added "so-called reality." That, however, was a very meager satisfaction; nor indeed did it satisfy Kingbitter.

Kingbitter, as he did frequently nowadays, was standing at his window and looking out onto the street below. This street offered the most mundane and ordinary sights of Budapest's mundane and ordinary streets. The muck-, oil-, and dog-dirt-spattered sidewalk was lined with parked cars, and in the one-yard gaps between the cars and the leprotically peeling house walls the most mundane and ordinary passersby were attempting to go about their business, their hostile features an outward clue to their dark thoughts. Every now and then, perhaps in a hurry to overtake the single file inching along in front, one of them would step off the sidewalk, only for an entire chorus of rancorous car horns to give the lie to any groundless hope of breaking free from the line.

On the benches in the square over the way, at least the benches not already stripped of their planks, were perched the homeless of the area, with their bundles, shopping bags, and plastic flasks. Above a bushy beard sprouted a knitted cap of carmine red, its dangling bobble merrily brushing the forbidding fuzz. A man wearing the battered cap of an officer of some nonexistent army was in a faded, buttonless heavy overcoat bound by a coy silk belt of gaudy floral design that had no doubt once belonged to a woman's housecoat. On bunioned female feet, peeking from beneath a pair of jeans, silvered evening shoes with worn-down heels; farther off, on a narrow strip of sparse turf, legs drawn up in catatonic inertness, sprawled a figure indistinguishable from a bundle of rags, laid out by alcohol or drugs, or maybe both.

As he looked at the down-and-outs, Kingbitter all at once became conscious that he was again looking at the down-and-outs. Without doubt, Kingbitter was nowadays lavishing far too much attention on the down-and-outs. He was quite capable of frittering away whole half hours of his (as it happened, worthless) time by the window, with the captivation of a voyeur who is completely unable to tear himself away from the obscene spectacle unfolding before him. On top of which, this Peeping Tom behavior was for Kingbitter attended by a sense of guilt and, at one and the same time, a loathsome attraction which debouched ultimately into a form of nauseating anguish or existential angst. The moment this anguish took unmistakable shape within him, Kingbitter, having attained as it were his baffling activity's even more baffling goal, would turn away from the window with almost an air of satisfaction and step toward the table, on which were strewn various manuscripts, opened and spread out like the carcasses of birds.

Kingbitter himself was well aware that there was something unsettling about this obsessive link that he had developed, one could say without his knowledge and consent, with the down-and-outs. In truth, he suffered from it as from an illness. All he needed to do was decide not to step toward the window anymore. Or to step toward the window solely in order to blow the cobwebs away or for some other practical purpose of that kind. But then, all at once, he would again catch himself at the window looking at the down-and-outs.

Kingbitter suspected that some intelligible meaning lay hidden behind this curious passion of his. Indeed, he had a feeling that if he were to succeed in deciphering that meaning, then he would also have a better understanding of his life, which he did not understand nowadays. He had a feeling as if nowadays rifts were separating him from that formerly almost palpable constant that he at some time had been acquainted with as his personality. For Kingbitter the Hamlet question did not run "To be or not to be?" but "Am I or am I not?"

Kingbitter leafed almost distractedly through one of the typescripts that was sprawled on the table. It was a fairly bulky pile of paper, the manuscript of a play. On the cover sheet stood the title, LIQUIDATION, then the designation of its genre: *Comedy in Three Acts.* Below that: *The setting is Budapest, in* 1990. He grasped the sheet between finger and thumb so as to turn the page, but then gave way nonetheless to the dubious pleasure bestowed by the stage directions:

(A dingy editorial office in a dingy publishing house. Shabby walls, sagging book stacks, yawning gaps between the books stowed on the shelves, dust, neglect; although there are no signs that a move is under way, the desolate impermanence of a moving operation prevails all around. In the room are four desks, four work

spaces. On each desk are a typewriter—a dust cover on one or two of them—piles of books, manuscript sheets, files. The windows overlook a courtyard. At the rear is a door leading to a corridor. Somewhere in the distance there is late-morning sunlight; in the dingy editorial office, dingy artificial lighting.

Kürti and his wife, Sarah, and Dr. Obláth are present in the room, ill at ease as they sit waiting around a desk that, as will become clear, belongs to Kingbitter.)

Kingbitter began to be seized by the passion to read on, the strange obsession that had so decisively shaped his life. He liked the play's opening exchanges.

KÜRTI: Abominable. Execrable. I could throw up. This building. A palace once, you know. Those stairs. This room. All this.

OBLÁTH *(to Sarah)*: Tell me, do you know what he's going on about?

SARAH: He's bored.

OBLÁTH: I'm also bored. You're also bored.

SARAH: But he's radically bored; that's the only radicalism he has now. That's what has been left him from the glory days. Boredom. He takes it with him everywhere, like an angry shaggy terrier that he sets on others from time to time.

KÜRTI: We were ordered to be here for eleven . . .

SARAH *(in a mollifying, almost pleading tone, as if speaking to a child)*: No one "ordered" us. Kingbitter asked us to bring the material into the office. By eleven, if possible.

KÜRTI: Eleven-thirty, and not a soul around. That doesn't bother you two, of course. You just sit there and tolerate it, the same way everything in this country is tolerated. Every deception, every lie, every bullet in the brains. Just as you are already tolerating bullets in the brains that will be implemented only after the bullet is put in your brains.

Kingbitter laughed out loud. Or, to be more precise, he heard the distinctive curt snort that nowadays passed for a laugh with him. The sound welled up, so to say, from the belly and came out more as a dry grunt than a laugh; to be sure, there was not much in the way of mirth and happiness tinkling in it. He leafed on in the manuscript until his eye was again caught by a stage direction:

(Kingbitter hurries in, a thick file under his arm.)

KINGBITTER: Do forgive me. It couldn't be helped. Sorry, sorry. The conference ran way overtime.

SARAH: You look stressed. Did something happen?

KINGBITTER: Nothing special; the publishing house is to be liquidated, that's all. The state is not going to throw money at the losses any longer. It has financed them for forty years; from today onward it is not going to finance them.

OBLÁTH: That's logical. It's another state now.

KÜRTI: The state is always the same. The only reason it financed literature up till now was in order to liquidate it. Giving state support to literature is the state's sneaky way for the state liquidation of literature.

OBLÁTH *(in ironic acknowledgment)*: An axiomatic formulation.

SARAH: And what is to become of the publishing house? Will it cease to exist?

KINGBITTER: In its present form. *(He shrugs, a bit dejectedly.)* But then, everything and everyone is ceasing to exist in its present form.

Yes, Kingbitter well recalled that morning nine years before. He recalled how, having come out of the editorial conference (the so-called editorial conference), a thick file under his arm, he had entered that room. Kürti, Sarah, and Obláth had been waiting for him there, by his desk. He himself had said near enough exactly what was in the play. The only snag was that by the time that scene was played out in reality, almost word for word, the person who had written the play, and that scene in it, was no longer alive.

He had committed suicide.

The police had found the syringe and the morphine ampoules as well.

Kingbitter had retained sufficient presence of mind to rescue the bulk of the manuscripts (a dazed Sarah had taken possession of the scanty correspondence) before the authorities arrived.

He had found this stage work too among the private

papers. A good nine years ago, when Kingbitter had first read the play, the story was only just beginning, and it had soon carried on, with the character the play called Kingbitter—exactly like the real-life Kingbitter—retaining sufficient presence of mind at the scene of the suicide to rescue the bulk of the manuscripts before the authorities arrived. Then, having secured the literary haul and greedily set upon it, Kingbitter had come across the stage work and, shortly afterward, the scene in which it turns out that he had retained sufficient presence of mind, et cetera. Thereafter, the scenes had succeeded one another, turn and turn about, in the drama as in reality, to the point that, in the end, Kingbitter did not know what to admire more: the author's—his dead friend's—crystal-clear foresight or his own, so to say, remorseful determination to identify with his prescribed role and stick to the story.

Nowadays, though, with the lapse of nine years, Kingbitter was interested in something else. His story had reached an end, but he himself was still here, posing a problem for which he more and more put off finding a solution. He would either have to carry on his story, which had proved impossible, or else start a new story, which had proved equally impossible. Kingbitter undoubtedly could see solutions to hand, both better ones and worse; indeed, if he reflected more deeply, solutions were all he could see, rather than lives. The character named Kürti in the play, for instance, had nowadays opted for the solution of falling ill. The last time Kingbitter paid a visit to him, he had found him in bed, surrounded by a sphygmomanometer, a little table on which were tablets of varied hues and shapes, packs of medicines, even a tiny gadget with which Kürti could self-inject; Sarah was sitting apathetically in the kitchen. This Kürti had once been a sociologist, retreating into some insignificant job during the seventies and eighties and meanwhile writing with unflagging zest his big monograph "on untimely consciousness and its cognitive roots in Hungary." Prior to that he had even done time in prison, and though the secret police were no longer beating prisoners by then, they had still managed to land a blow so wretchedly that he had gone deaf in his left ear.

Kingbitter leafed back a few sheets in the play. We are back again at the opening scene, with Kürti, his wife, Sarah, and Dr. Obláth waiting for him, Kingbitter. Obláth says something, Kürti does not understand him, and Obláth repeats it at the top of his lungs.

SARAH: There's no need to yell. Just don't speak into his battered ear.

OBLÁTH *(awkwardly apologetic)*: I always forget!

KÜRTI *(who has meanwhile set off on a walk around the room, inspects the bookshelves and furnishings, picks out a book or two)*: Better you do. It was all over and done with long ago. *(He rummages tentatively among the books, seeming to speak more or less in a trance.)* And strangely enough, it all came to an end just recently. Quite suddenly. Just when it was in the home stretch.

The régime was overthrown, and I'm not going to pretend it was me who overthrew it. A general liquidation is in full swing, and I'm not going to join in. I've become a spectator. And I'm not even spectating from the front rows in the stalls but from somewhere up in the gods. Maybe I'm worn out, but it could be that I never truly believed in what I believed. That would be the unseemlier alternative, because then they would have smashed my ear in for no reason at all. That is the assumption I'm inclining to these days. *(He breaks off and ponders, book in hand.)* I did time for no reason, dragged the millstone of a police record around for no reason, was on probation for years for no reason, and I'm no hero, I merely botched up my life.

OBLÁTH *(consolingly)*: Everyone here makes a botch of his life. That's the local specialty, the genius loci. Anyone who doesn't botch up his life here simply has no talent.

Kingbitter again heard the laugh that sounded more like an irate snort than a laugh. He regretted that he had missed that scene (he recalled that he had entered the room only later, with the thick file under his arm) and so had been unable to take part in the conversation. He liked the style, that wry gallows humor armed with the semblance of omniscience; a most serviceable style it was, the dialect of the initiated, protecting them from their disillusionments, their fears, their well-concealed childish hopes.

13

Kingbitter looked at his watch and established that he had nothing at all to do that day either. It was slowly getting on for noon. He fleetingly wondered how he had spent his day so far, but he would have been hard put to give an answer to that. True, he had been living a lively interior life today: he had dreamed something, he had awoken with an erection, and while shaving he had been dogged by a feeling that today he needed to decide, though he could not see clearly what it was he needed to decide, besides which he was all too aware of his own inability to make any decisions.

Despite that, the thought did cross Kingbitter's mind that he ought to do something about finding a theater to do the play, the comedy (or tragedy?) "Liquidation."

He was now in the ninth year of considering that.

Indeed, Kingbitter was now in the ninth year of considering whether he was handling the literary estate with due diligence.

There were all sorts of things in the legacy: prose pieces and notes, diary extracts and embryonic short stories (and the play *Liquidation,* of course). It was just that a crucial bit was missing—or at least so Kingbitter was convinced.

Apart from which—and this was Kingbitter's most secret thought, so secret that he maybe kept it a secret even from himself—if he were to be rid of the play, he would, in some sense, also be getting rid of himself. He might also be rid of the oppressive sense of implausibility that stuck to him nowadays, haunting him like some disagreeable deficiency, at all times and in all places, like Peter Schlemihl and his missing shadow.

The story had begun on that morning when Kingbitter, thick file under his arm, had entered the publishing office where Kürti, his wife, Sarah, and Dr. Obláth were waiting for him.

In the file in question was the literary estate of Kingbitter's dead friend—let's call him B. for short (or Bee, as he liked to call himself). The way the estate had come into Kingbitter's hands was that Kingbitter had retained sufficient presence of mind to rescue the bulk of the manuscripts before . . . but he has already had occasion to mention that.

Kingbitter had appeared at the editorial conference (the so-called editorial conference) that morning, file under his arm, with the firm intention of recommending that the publishing house, of which he was one of the literary editors, publish the legacy, and offering himself to undertake the editorial work relating to publication (forgoing any fees, naturally).

Except that the conference had been convened in order to announce the sad fact that the publishing house was operating at a loss, and for that reason they would be obliged to undertake certain administrative and financial maneuvers, from the stupefyingly tedious analysis of which all that Kingbitter grasped—but grasped with utter clarity—was that he would be ill advised to bring up the matter of his recommendation at this moment in time.

He again began to take an interest in what they had actually been talking about before he, having left the so-called conference, entered the room where his friends were awaiting him.

Obláth has just been discoursing on something in his habitual, passionately high-flown manner, his words followed by a prolonged hush. Sarah is sniffling, occasionally raising her handkerchief to dab her reddened eyes; Kürti drags his chair a bit farther away and wraps himself in a detached, profound silence.

OBLÁTH *(noticing that the other two are barely paying any attention, quickly wraps up his soliloquy)*: . . . So, ever since then I have been haunted by the thought that perhaps—who could know?—he may have committed philosophical suicide. Like a Dostoyevsky character, let's say. I could imagine that—of him, definitely I could.

(Hush.)

OBLÁTH: Fine, I'll take that back.

(Hush.)

OBLÁTH: It just crossed my mind.

(Hush.)

OBLÁTH: Because we don't know anything as it is. In my case, not even . . . well, not even exactly how he . . .

(Hush. Kürti scrutinizes his wife's face, but Sarah remains silent.)

KÜRTI: Sarah will tell you.

SARAH: With drugs.

OBLÁTH: You've already told me that much. Sleeping pills?

SARAH *(evasively)*: I don't know. When they called me into the police station . . .

OBLÁTH *(astonished)*: You were called into the police station?

KÜRTI: Sarah had a key to the apartment.

SARAH: It wasn't me who had a key. Kingbitter had a key. *(Kürti nods vigorously with a wry smile, as if he does not believe a word Sarah is saying.)*

SARAH: Look, Sándor, wouldn't it just be simpler if we got a divorce?

KÜRTI: Simpler, yes indeed.

SARAH: Then why don't we divorce?

KÜRTI: But why? It's just as nonsensical as staying together. To say nothing of all the inconvenience.

Whoosh!—the letters slipped away from Kingbitter's gaze in a flash, as if devoured by fire. Kingbitter had also typed the play into his computer so that he could read it alternately, now on-screen, now in typescript, though he preferred most of all to read the autograph manuscript, which was also extant in the legacy, in B.'s untidy yet for Kingbitter readily legible handwriting. Character sketches, supplementary remarks, reminders, notes, and descriptions had been produced for each scene, though the definitive dialogues that had emerged from the notes barely differed from these notes, or the latter from the reality (that is to say, so-called reality), that is, the questionable and confused agglomeration of images, words, and events stored in Kingbitter's memory.

"Act 1. Single locality, four characters: KINGBITTER, SARAH, KÜRTI, OBLÁTH. What brings them together? A shared past, and their links with B. The fortuitousness of both factors. The past as a random collectivity of fates tossed together onto a heap with a pitchfork. As a shared world whose shameful secret they jointly preserve. They have never spelled it out yet, and they will always refrain from spelling it out. The static world of lives in suspense, besmirched by frail hope time and time again. That is not how they see it, however; they merely preserve a dim memory of the struggle, the way, day by day, they fought tooth and nail against barriers that were considered impregnable, until, all of a sudden—wonder of wonders—the resistance ceased, and they suddenly found themselves in a void that, in their initial dazed state, they imagined to be freedom.

In that regard, irrespective of their grief, B.'s suicide comes as a blow to them: the news of his death is like a jeering and unchallengeable rebuttal. They cautiously guess at the reasons for it. According to Obláth it is a matter of philosophy—of a radically negative disposition, a "ruthlessly applied" logic that in the end leads to depression, self-destruction, physical and mental degradation. Compared with B., says Obláth, he, Obláth, doctor of philosophy, who pursues philosophy professionally and from a university chair, is a rank beginner.

True, he had never claimed to be an original thinker. "If I were, maybe they would long ago have smashed my ear too, or my kidneys, or whatever they are in the habit of smashing," he says, obviously paying tribute to Kürti. He mentions that he and B., a few years before, had done a lot of intensive philosophizing: they had both been at a "creative writers' retreat," as institutions of the kind were known at the time. They had strolled on the late-autumn leaf mold, conducting peripatetic deliberations under bloated plane trees.

"We took big walks in the woods," recalls Obláth, who is fond of epic preambles. "He expounded that there were no tragic individuals anymore. You probably heard that theory from him yourselves. But there, in the Mátra Hills, he was unusually lucid. Man, when reduced to nothing, or in other words a *survivor,* is not tragic but comic, because he has no fate. On the other hand, he lives with an awareness of tragic fate. This is a paradox [*pa-waadox,* in Obláth's affected diction], which manifests itself in him, the writer, simply as a problem of style. A striking notion, I have to say," he adds with the smile of approbation that he was clearly in the habit of awarding the more polished essays at the university. "In his classification, survivors represent a separate species," he continues, "just like an animal species. In his view, we are all survivors; that is what determines our perverse and degenerate mental world. Auschwitz. Then the forty years that we have put behind us since. He said that he had not yet discovered a precise answer to this latter-day deformation of survival—those forty years, that is to say—but he was looking for it and was already close to the mark."

He falls silent, pausing briefly for effect.

"That is why I entertain the idea of philosophical suicide," he says eventually. "Maybe he decided that was the answer." Adding swiftly, "*His* answer, at any rate."

The others are not much inclined to agree.

Kürti:
"He didn't live like someone who was preparing to commit suicide. He was a connoisseur of life, in his own way."

Obláth:
"A connoisseur of life? Don't take this the wrong way, but that calls for amplification."

Kürti:
"He avoided participation of any kind, never became mixed up in anything, didn't believe, didn't revolt, and didn't become disillusioned."

Obláth:
"One could also add that he was barely domiciled, never traveled, and harbored not a drop of ambition. Even so, I may still be right."

Kürti:
"He remained an innocent, like an old maid."

Obláth:
"I would rather phrase it that no one navigated those forty years as elegantly as he did. He floated like . . . like a . . ." He falls silent.

What he wanted to say was: He floated like a phantom albatross of unspotted whiteness on the ice gray ocean. But he conceded that he had no way of justifying the simile. He had been reading *Moby-Dick* the previous evening, before falling asleep.

They inevitably soon reverted to the matter of the police. Obláth knows nothing at all about this. Whom had they called in? Why? What key were they talking about? The key to B.'s apartment. Kingbitter had a key, as it happened. Really! Obláth marvels. The prince of intellectuals dished out keys to his apartment? Yes, says Kingbitter. He himself had been surprised at B.'s uncustomary confidence. B. had wanted him to sort out his manuscripts for publication. He had invited Kingbitter to the apartment and shown him where he kept the papers. He had given him a free hand: he should pick and grub around in them as he saw fit. Kingbitter had been deeply touched; he had always longed to be able to do that, because he wanted B. to publish more. He had secretly hoped that he would come across a novel in the drawer. Now, sadly, B.'s real intentions were plain: he had merely wished to make provisions for his literary estate. Yes, plainly, says Obláth. It was Kingbitter who had reported the death, was it not? Yes, it was. And what had they wanted from Sarah? Who knows? says Kingbitter. In his initial floundering he had rung Kürti, but Kürti happened not to be home, so he had asked Sarah to come out to B.'s apartment. Why? Obláth is amazed. Because in his initial panic he had felt unable to endure being alone in the apartment, with B.'s corpse, for even a moment. The other residents of the house "had seen a woman," which was why Sarah had also been called in, but the matter was quickly cleared up. While this conversation is in progress, Kürti noisily opens a newspaper and demonstratively engrosses himself in it, as if he had nothing to do with the conversation. And what had they really wanted from Kingbitter? "Nothing. Bloody fools," says Kingbitter.

(Kingbitter crosses to the other side of the stage, which is suddenly illuminated. A desk, behind which the INSPECTOR *is seated.)*

INSPECTOR: You reported the death at around four p.m., but someone saw you in the building at around ten o'clock that morning.

KINGBITTER *(nervously)*: All that was already in my statement.

INSPECTOR: Yes, the one made at the scene. Now we need to close the file, however. I'm asking for your assistance. So, you spent some twenty to twenty-five minutes in the apartment without reporting the death.

KINGBITTER: I wasn't aware that he was dead. I didn't notice anything out of the ordinary. I thought he was asleep.

INSPECTOR: How did you get into the apartment?

KINGBITTER: With a key, and I know what you're going

to ask next. *(Stuttering)* I got the key from him; he almost forced it on me. I suppose that for his sense of security he wanted . . .

INSPECTOR: Is that what he told you?

KINGBITTER: Not in so many words, but—

INSPECTOR *(interrupting)*: What did he say, then? Why did he want you to have a key to his apartment?

KINGBITTER *(becoming a bit flustered)*: How can I put it . . . He made a joke of it. He said, "Let there be one key with you, seeing you're so happy rifling through my drawers."

INSPECTOR: He said that?

KINGBITTER: Yes.

INSPECTOR: Hmmm, I see . . . So tell me, please, what exactly you did in the apartment from the moment you entered . . . *(he lays out a sheet of paper on the desk, then turns it round toward Kingbitter, presumably so he may see it better)* . . . here.

KINGBITTER: What's this?

INSPECTOR: A plan of the apartment. One and a half rooms in a housing project high-rise. The main room is here, on the right; those there, on the left, are the bathroom and the spare room, with the kitchen opposite. That is the entrance hall . . .

KINGBITTER *(poring over the drawing)*: That's right.

INSPECTOR: So? What do you do?

KINGBITTER: I'm preparing, let me think, to greet him with a "Good morning" or something of the sort, when I see that he is asleep—

INSPECTOR: Dead.

KINGBITTER: You know that now, but I didn't know it myself at the time. The bed was over against the wall; all I could see was the back of his head and the duvet.

INSPECTOR: Fair enough, but when you entered the room—

KINGBITTER: I didn't enter the room.

INSPECTOR: Where did you go, then?

KINGBITTER: To the spare room. That's where his writing desk was; that's where he kept his files.

INSPECTOR: And what did you do there?

KINGBITTER: What he had asked me to do when he gave me the key. I went through his papers.

INSPECTOR: And did you take anything away?

KINGBITTER *(looks slightly alarmed now)*: The very idea! I didn't touch a thing.

INSPECTOR: So where are the papers now?

KINGBITTER: What papers?

INSPECTOR: The ones you didn't touch.

KINGBITTER: Precisely! Where are they?

(Silence. Kingbitter and the Inspector mutely take measure of each other. There is a barely perceptible smile on Kingbitter's face, as if he is even enjoying the game a little.)

INSPECTOR: Do you know anything about the tattoo?

KINGBITTER: The what?

INSPECTOR: The deceased bore a distinctive mark on his thigh. Do you know about it?

KINGBITTER: Of course I do . . . Or rather . . . *(he completely loses his composure)*. What did you say? A distinctive what?

INSPECTOR *(in a listless monotone, as if all of a sudden he has grown weary of making inquiries, of his profession, of life itself, of everything)*: I'm talking about a tattoo, Mr. Kingbitter. A very visible, greenish blue tattoo on the outside of the thigh.

Kingbitter shakes his head.

INSPECTOR: A capital letter *B* and then a four-digit number.

Kingbitter still none the wiser.

INSPECTOR: I spoke with the pathologist. Elderly man. *(He hesitates before letting the word out in a rush.)* Jewish. Exactly like an Auschwitz prisoner number, he says, except in that case it would not be on the thigh but the forearm. Interesting, wouldn't you say?

KINGBITTER: Yes, very interesting, only I haven't the slightest idea about the numbering of Auschwitz prisoners, and anyway, I'm not Jewish.

INSPECTOR *(makes a brisk hand gesture, as if brushing off a fly)*: That's neither here nor there as far as I'm concerned.

KINGBITTER: Why is the tattoo so important?

INSPECTOR: It might be a lead to certain circles . . . We would be interested to know, for instance, where he acquired the morphine.

KINGBITTER *(startled)*: So, it was morphine . . . ?

INSPECTOR: Didn't you know? We made a search of the apartment. The ampoules were found under the pillow. Regular hospital-supply ampoules, and along with those a syringe taken from a sterile pack. Ordinary addicts make do with used syringes. *(A momentary pause.)* Are you acquainted with any doctor or other health care worker among his close friends who you suppose might have been able to help the deceased gain access to the poison?

KINGBITTER: No idea.

INSPECTOR: Do you know his ex-wife?

KINGBITTER: Sure I do. It's been at least five years since they divorced . . . Why do you ask?

INSPECTOR: No reason in particular. I just happened to check what his wife's occupation is. Physician.

KINGBITTER *(taken aback)*: Well, what of it?

INSPECTOR: That's all. Still, just a tiny bit interesting, wouldn't you say?

KINGBITTER *(groping for words in his amazement)*: I don't understand what could be of any interest about that . . .

(Lights dim.

When the lights come up again, they are all sitting in the same places as before.)

Sarah, fighting back her tears, asks Kingbitter why he had actually kept the detective in the dark about the truth, that he was aware of the tattoo and its significance.

Kingbitter rejoins that in that case he would have had to relate B.'s entire life history to the detective.

Right. And why had he not done so?

For some reason he just couldn't face going into it, says Kingbitter.

Sure, but why not?

"I've racked my brains a lot about that myself," said Kingbitter.

I'VE RACKED MY BRAINS A LOT ABOUT THAT myself. The circumstances go a long way to providing an explanation. How could I have related B.'s story to a policeman? What kind of police language would the policeman have used to record B.'s story, that truly untellable story, in a statement? There I was, sitting in a stuffy office room, in the light of naked lamp bulbs, sitting opposite an indifferent official's gaze, eyeglasses, lackluster hair, lackluster eyes; when I entered the room he shook hands with me, and the palm of his hand was clammy. In what language could I have told him B.'s story? Objectively? Dramatically? Statement-like, if I may put it that way?

It was a ghastly moment, because I realized that B. had lived with that story as long as he lived, and, I suppose, I realized what it must have meant to live with that story. There, in that office room, where, so I felt, all the world's indifference was concentrated—there I realized that every story had come to an end, that all our stories are untellable stories, and he, B., was the only person who, in his own way, the way he always used to, which is to say radically, had drawn the resulting conclusion.

That was why I had to go after his vanished novel. Because it probably contained everything I needed to know, everything that can still be known at all.

27

Only from our stories can we discover that our stories have come to an end, otherwise we would go on living as if there were still something for us to continue (our stories, for example); that is, we would go on living in error.

B. at least had a story, even if that story was untellable and incomprehensible.

I don't have even that much. If I wish to see my life as a story (and who would not wish to be acquainted with his own story so he may then, his mind eased—or for that matter, uneased—call it his fate?), then I would have to tell the story of B.

I shall indeed have a shot at giving a short summary of that story—the story of B., that is—or at least its beginnings, its genesis, if I may put it that way; that is to say, all that needs to be known about the tattooing and that I could not tell the policeman, or anyone else for that matter, because I considered it to be an untellable story.

As indeed it is.

It may be easier for me to tell it if I return to the original situation, the fatuous questions and the even more fatuous answers: the way we, persons who with B.'s disappearance had all at once been left without stories, attempted to interpret that story.

To be brief: There we were, sitting in the publishing office, sitting there, the four of us, who after all had something to do with B. and his story; indeed, except for the objective Dr. Obláth, who in true philosopher's fashion had created for himself his own continuable, one might say infinitely continuable, impartial philosophy sor's story—so, we who had not only been admitted into B.'s story but on whom that story had moreover wreaked a greater or lesser degree of havoc.

The reason I had originally asked them there, to the publishing house, was that I had asked each of them for an essay, some sort of brief foreword, for the volume that was to be assembled from B.'s literary estate, and I had hoped that day to be able to hand over the already drawn-up contracts, maybe even a requisition for a modest advance. At that point, I was not to know what I got to know that morning at the so-called editorial conference, namely, that our woebegone publishing house was operating at a loss, and on that account I would be better advised not even to come forward with my recommendation relating to publication of B.'s legacy.

I beg my own pardon for being constrained to put down claptrap like this on paper; only now do I see how difficult it must be for my clients, so-called (or perchance genuine) writers, to wrestle with unvarnished matter, objective reality, the entire phenomenological world, in order to reach the essence that glimmers behind it—that is, if any such thing exists, of course. In most cases, one sets off from the premise that it does exist, because one is unable to reconcile oneself to the inessentiality of one's life, though I fear that is the true situation, *the existential condition,* as Dr. Obláth, that amiable booby, would put it.

There we were, then, sitting and holding our peace, as we were all familiar enough with B.'s untellable story.

As best I recall, in the end it was I who spoke first:

"What blithering idiots they are! They notice the tattoo, but they don't think to check the place and date of birth."

That splendid fellow Kürti, who was not exactly in the most sparkling of moods that day—and with good reason, too—remarked that if I thought they had really not checked those data, then it was I who was the blithering idiot; on the other hand, of course, the authorities were also blithering idiots, but only, so to say, authoritatively blithering idiots in not seeing a link between the two things, or not even considering there might be a link.

Now, to come finally to the point, B. was born in the last month of 1944 at Oswiecim, to be quite precise in one of the barracks of Birkenau, within the concentration camp better known as Auschwitz.

Obláth remarked that he regarded it as conceivable that the congruence of the place-names Auschwitz and Oswiecim had not even occurred to the police. That was something we all would have to agree on, given the devastating lack of education, the inanity, barbarity, and villainy, and the rampant prevalence and official endorsement of all that in our country—albeit only offhand and apathetically, so to say, as if we had long ago lost any intention of ameliorating public life or altering anything. For if that were not the case, then the tattoo that was visible on the thigh would not have seemed so puzzling either, because then it would have been recognized that the few infants who were born in Auschwitz in the course of its history had a prison number tattooed on their thigh, since it could not be inscribed on an infant's arm, simply because an infant's arm was too short.

On the few occasions when I managed to corner him, B., who did not talk willingly, to put it mildly, about the circumstances of his birth, did tell me that the reason he had been given a four-digit number with the letter *B* was that his mother was entered into the hospital barracks' card file as a Slovak political prisoner; in addition, I learned from him that to the best of his knowledge, as he said, the forearms of Hungarian prisoners were generally tattooed with a letter *A* and a five- or six-digit number, and the chances of its being on the thigh of a Hungarian Jewish prisoner—that is, of an infant being saved—were effectively nil (those were his exact words).

As to how he had nevertheless managed to remain alive after that, I was able to extract only a few fragmentary bits of information. It may be he himself did not know much more. I don't imagine that he knew his mother and father; even if he did, he never spoke about them. I know nothing at all about his childhood either—merely that he ran away from an orphanage for boys. I saw that he had another name only when I had to draw up publisher's contracts in connection with his translations. "He loathed the name that he was given by his forefathers, just as he loathed his forefathers and all who gave rise to his existence," he once said. I made a note of the sentence. Interesting that I should have made notes about him—or maybe not all that interesting.

Reconstructing all the bits that I ended up gathering from him and others, I can build up roughly the following story. At the selection on entering the camp, either the medical selector does not notice that the woman (B.'s mother) is four months pregnant (which is conceivable) or else the pregnancy is not yet evident at all (which is likewise conceivable), though just possibly the pregnancy was indeed evident but we are dealing with a kind-natured medical selector (that too is conceivable, in the final analysis). The real problems would start a month or so later, with B.'s mother's body dwindling from day to day whereas her belly would be ever more apparent. Finally, she decides to act, although she probably knows only too well that she will be risking her own life: On some pretext (by citing, let us say, the involvement of her leg by a so-called phlegmon, one of those suppurating inflammatory lesions that counted as a run-of-the-mill ailment in the concentration camps), she gets her name onto the sick list for entry into the hospital barracks. That might mean certain death: Selections were routinely carried out among those reporting for the hospital barracks. On this occasion, though, there is no selection (that is an assumption on my part, for if there had been a selection, how else would the woman have gotten into the hospital barracks, as she undoubtedly did?). What followed can be traced with more precision. The hospital barracks *blokova,* or senior inmate, was a Polish female prisoner. B.'s mother was a native of Slovakia and could communicate superbly with the Polish *blokova:* that is a prerequisite for the whole thing. A few days later she discloses the in any case obvious secret. The *blokova,* possibly stirred by the thought of helping bring a child into the world in the death camp, and anyway maintaining far-flung contacts with mysterious authorities in the main camp, instantly sets to work. The camp is already being liquidated, order is breaking down: a Jewish woman's death is reported, a long-deceased Slovak female political prisoner is resurrected with the assistance of the camp administration—no great matter in Auschwitz, where lives are obliterated at the flick of a finger. The mother gives birth to her child in the hospital barracks, and the child, although instantly taken away from her, somehow manages to remain alive.

"A ghastly story," B. commented, "but it doesn't necessarily mean you have to drag it around with you at all times, like your wallet or I.D. card. You can dump it anywhere, forget it in a coffee bar or toss it away in the street, like some inconvenient parcel that you have been given by a stranger. After all, even the so-called normal circumstances of birth are none too edifying, if you think about it. One can never help being born."

I was stupid enough to encourage him to write it down.

"You don't know what you're talking about," he responded.

I suppose I really didn't know.

"It's fine the way it is," he continued, "shapeless and bloody, like a placenta. But once I write it down, it becomes a story. Discerning editor that you are, how would you assess a story like that?"

I held my tongue.

"Come on, now," he urged, "out with it."

"I don't know," I said.

"The hell you don't," he fumed. "Look here, I submit to you a piece concerning how, with the cooperation of a bunch of thoroughly decent people, a child is born in Auschwitz. The *Kapos* lay down their clubs and whips, and, moved to the core, they lift the wailing infant on high. Tears rise to the eyes of the SS guard."

"If you put it like that, then of course . . ."

"Huh?" he urged. "Huh?"

"Well . . . kitsch," I said. "But it can also be written in other ways," I added hastily.

"It can't. Kitsch is kitsch."

"But it's what happened," I protested.

That's precisely the problem, he explained. It happened, yet it's still not true. An exception, an anecdote. A speck of grit gets into the corpse-mincing machine. Who cared about his life, he said, exceptional only courtesy of the camp's Prominents, an anomalous, one-off industrial accident? And where does the nonexistent exceptional success story of this person called B. find a place in universal grand history?

Back then, right at the start of our acquaintance, I did not really understand what he was talking about. It may be I still don't understand him sufficiently. But conversations like that, in this icy gray city, mired in obtuse tedium and doltish resignation as it was, gradually began to cast a spell on me, as if I were recognizing in them a very distant, impossible dream of mine.

A QUESTION NOW ARISES. HOW CAN ONE BE A Persian? a French philosopher once inquired. How can one be a literary editor? is what I inquire. Or at least, how does one become a literary editor? A painter, a musician, or a writer, let's say—a person is usually born to be that. But a publisher's reader—hardly. It probably calls for some peculiar atrophy, and in order for me to grasp what that is, I would have to start a long way back. I would have to tell the story of my career, that is to say of my total depravation, the story of the depravation of my family (the Kesselbach family, who are reputed to have originally come from Switzerland to settle here), my social class, my milieu, my city, my country—the entire world. Being an incorrigible publisher's reader, head brimming with sentences picked up at random from all corners of world literature, I am immediately drawn to think of a book, a possible beginning: *It is by no means out of any wish to bring my own personality into the foreground that I preface with a few words about myself and my own affairs this report on the story of the departed B.* . . . Or should that be, the *life*? Even, the *life story*?

How did I come by that book, which, as will become clear by and by, exerted such a distressing influence on my undoubtedly somewhat ridiculous realm of fantasy? There was no literature in my family. No art. I grew up among sensible people whom wars and various dictatorships had formed into—what indeed? I might more accurately formulate it if I were to say: I grew up among sober people whose minds, character, and individuality had been liquidated by wars and various dictatorships. As I have mentioned, the family was Swiss in origin; by dint of cattle dealing, pursued uninterruptedly during the sixteenth and seventeenth centuries, even in the midst of Turkish occupation and other vicissitudes, they struck roots in Transylvania . . .

Maybe not. Let's drop that. A few points of purchase will do. It was Grandpa who liquidated the Kesselbach name, during the First World War. Since the poor man had just lost his elder, favorite son at the front, and since it was advisable, but also practically expedient, to retain the initial letter (incredible as it may seem, people wore monogrammed underwear in those days), he chose the name Kingbitter, because he lived in bitterness. During the Second World War my father moved from Transylvania to Budapest, because he feared retribution from . . . (it hardly matters what I might write in place of those three dots: the Romanians, the Russians, the communists, the Jews, the Nazis, Habsburg loyalists, the socialists). In Budapest, as so-called Transylvanian refugees, the family was housed in a Jewish apartment that had been looted and vacated not long before. Immediately after the battle of Budapest, my father fretted about making a further run for it, as he again had reason to fear retribution, this time from the original owners of the apartment. The owners did not put in an appearance, however, from which it could be deduced that, luckily, they had been exterminated. Father set considerable weight on that formulation. Later on, as a child, I myself heard it that way from his own lips.

"Never put a gloss on the truth," he would instruct the family. "Don't accept ready-made cheap words. Let us at least keep our nerve; that can't be nationalized. Look facts in the face: The reason we are able to live here, the reason we have any dwelling at all, is because, *luckily,* the original owners were exterminated. Otherwise we would have nowhere to live. There you are . . . that's Hungarian luck for you," he added (*nomen est omen*) bitterly.

I loved my father. He had a handsome gray careworn face, handsome gray careworn eyes. Occasionally, conversation at home turned to an older, grander life, some time long ago and somewhere else, but when I knew my father he was a so-called legal clerk for a so-called state enterprise. "Intellectual vegetation"—that is how, with a tiny grimace and tiny hand gesture, he characterized his unacceptable occupation, which he must have accepted all the same as he pursued it on a daily basis. I did not experience the supposedly obligatory fate of a boy rebelling against the father. There was no one and nothing for me to rebel against: my rebellious dynamic would have cracked straightaway on my father's nonexistent, long-crushed resistance.

Why am I recording all this? I don't know, because none of it goes to show a thing. In the world as it presented itself to me, effects did not always derive from causes, nor did causes always prove adequately grounded points of departure; as a result, in that world the sort of logic that presumed to arrive at causes through unraveling the effects was a mistaken logic. I consider that the world as it presented itself to me had no logic whatsoever.

The fact is that in my nineteenth or twentieth year—it was the early sixties by then—a book came into my hands. I think I mentioned this book earlier, though I shall not identify either title or author here, because names and the perceptions that accrete to them have a different significance for everyone in every era. I knew about the existence of this book only from other books, in the way that an astronomer infers the existence of an unknown celestial body from the motion of other planets; yet in those days, the era of undiscoverable reasons, it was not possible to get hold of it for some undiscoverable reason. I happened to be grinding through university at the time; though I did not have much money, I staked it all on the venture, mobilizing antiquarian booksellers, denying myself meals in order to acquire an old edition. I then read the bulky volume in less than three days, sitting on a bench in the public garden of a city square, as spring was in the air outside while a constant, depressing gloom reigned within my sublet room. I recall to this day the adventures of the imagination that I lived through at the time while I read in the book that the Ninth Symphony had been withdrawn. I felt privileged, like someone who had become privy to a secret reserved for few; like someone who had been suddenly awakened in order to have the world's irredeemable condition revealed to him, all at once, in the blinding light of a judgment.

Still, I don't think it was that book which carried me into my fateful career. I finished reading it; then, like all the others, it gradually died down within me under the dense, soft layers of my subsequent reading matter. Masses of books, good and bad, of all sorts of genres are dormant within me. Sentences, words, paragraphs, and lines of poetry that, like restless subtenants, unexpectedly spring to life and wander solitarily about or at other times launch into a loud chattering that I am unable to quell. An occupational hazard. While editing a world-famous conductor's world-famous memoirs, I chanced upon what may presumably have even been a true sentence: The conductor was complaining that as a result of intensive rehearsals he was suffering from chronic insomnia because he was unable to master the constant orchestral din swirling around in his head.

No, a person becomes a literary editor, and later a publisher's reader, out of error in the first place. In any event, literature is the trap that captures him. To be more precise, reading: reading as a narcotic which pleasantly blurs the merciless outlines of the life that holds sway over us. It started, perhaps, somewhere in university—with university friendships, in the course of those mammoth, deep, and meaningless conversations that stretch far into the night. A friend suddenly publishes a poem. Prior to that he had happened to hand it over for you to read, and you had dropped some great profundity regarding one of the couplets. In time, people get into the habit of regularly asking your opinion. You bustle self-importantly along corridors, a sheaf of other people's manuscripts pinned under your arm. A fastidiousness of some kind evolves within you, some kind of mental hygiene that is deemed infallible taste. The word gets around that you "have a bent for literature," as they say, and in the end you believe it yourself. You become editor of the university magazine. Under the conditions of censorship, you learn how to strike a balance, which, at the time, hapless wretch that you are, you regard as a fun game to play. Occasionally, you receive secret pats on the back "for your balls." Later, you go on to acquire that effortless cynicism, prevalent within publishing houses, in which you delight. Around that time there was still such a thing as the fresh smell of printer's ink, and one could even come across an older writer who still submitted his works for publication, by the state's grace, in handwriting.

What am I blathering on about here? Before you know it I'll be launching into anecdotes. Only now can I see how hard it is to keep to the clear structure, subtle thematic development, and consistent style that distinguish a true writer from dilettantes like myself. I need to investigate the passion—the sole true, great passion in my life, I should say—that, as time went by, degenerated into a mania, the object of which, naturally, was a book: in this case a missing book, B.'s vanished novel. Was? It may still come to light even today, though I don't put much faith in that. Why, then, do I think of it as some incontrovertible fact? Why do I think that B. wrote this novel, notwithstanding the fact that no one has ever seen the manuscript, and everyone denies its existence? Well, I for one am certain that he did write it. He could not have departed without writing it, because he was a writer, a true writer, and writers complete their works, whether those be thousands of pages long or just a few laconic lines. Great writers don't leave unfinished works behind; that much I have learned over the course of my career. It would be vitally important for me to read it, because I would probably learn from it why he died, and perhaps also whether, now that he is dead, it is permissible—if I may put it this way—for me to go on living.

I am trying to think when our friendship began to shift more into a form of dependence—I mean my dependence, of course, since Bee was as independent as an icicle (in both the injurious and ephemeral senses of the word, as I see now in hindsight)—until I became embroiled in his story to the point that I have been unable to separate it from my own ever since. I suppose it all began with the conversation we had, not long after I was released from prison, in the farthest corner of a dimly lit café. Not that he was entirely uninvolved in the circumstances that had led to my being arrested in the first place—by which, needless to say, I am thinking purely of abstract matters, solely of the intellectual influence that he exercised over me from the very first moment. When I think harder about it, something else must also have happened: That certain book which was lying dormant within me also secretly awakened. My work as a publisher's reader was never completely fulfilling, not even in the glory days when, alone or in league with short-term allies, I managed to steer a book that I was enthusiastic about, let us say, or publication of which I simply considered to be important, through the ever-vigilant height of nonsense that was censorship. Also slumbering within me, it seems, together with the book, was a figure (and perhaps also a complementary figure, but best not go into that) that all of a sudden sprang into life when B. came along, like Lohengrin lying unawakened in Elsa. If I carry on like this, however, I fear that I would be stepping onto very shaky ground. Never mind. My life lacked the type of artist for whom a person would in fact embark on a career as a publisher's reader. A poète maudit—there, I've said it now, however infantile it may sound.

I can't help it, but everyone has his so-called ideal, even though it is not done to talk about it, and even though everyone denies it. I saw a man who lived by his own rules; time wore on, and before I knew it, I caught myself living parasitically off his words—taking my cue from him, needing to know what he was thinking and doing, what he was working on. Does that sound too silly? But then that's what we're like, somewhat second-hand people, feeding off the lives of those stronger than ourselves, as though a crumb of those lives is our due as well. I was in deep trouble at that time, both ethically and in other respects (to be brief: my life, lying in ruins as it was anyway, seemed to be falling apart), and in the acuteness of my vulnerability I was ready to accept any influence. Those were dark days; it was winter in the city, winter in my heart. I was entertaining very serious thoughts of doing away with myself. The capacity to endow my life with a notion of sense simply deserted me. As I saw it, my life was costing me far too much grief as compared with any joy that it was still able to furnish. That was when I became acquainted with the view Bee had formed about suicide; it was a startlingly original view, in flat contradiction to the act that he carried out in the end all the same.

I sense, though, that I am starting to become difficult to follow. Maybe I should return to some kind of chronology—to relate, for instance, how I came to meet Bee, only I no longer recollect that. Everyone in the publishing house knew Bee. I was then working in the literary readers' department and had nothing to do with B., whose dealings were with the editors of foreign-language literature (he translated from French, English, and German with equal brilliance). I nevertheless noticed him because Bee was a strident, jolly figure, agreeably diverting and tremendously witty—that was the garb in which he clothed himself every morning. I could not have known that at the time; at all events, I found him a little off-putting. There came a day nonetheless when we fell into conversation in the cafeteria, that socialist haven of morning-after flapjacks, dubious sandwiches, and watery coffee, where everyone regularly dropped in from time to time, in search of momentary solace and refuge. Our publishing house, you see, had a supplement, a popular monthly magazine, for which I was one of the editors. That entailed a constant struggle for copy, which is how, accompanied by a morning-after flapjack and some ersatz marmalade, I came to ask B. whether, besides his translation work, he was in the habit of writing as well, and if he was, did he happen to have some original article for our magazine? It was then that I first saw his real face: he was capable of giving a very nasty look. "Who do you take yourself for?" he asked. I told him that I worked there, and I was under the apprehension that we had already met. "I don't mean that," he rejoined. He scrutinized me sternly for a while. "Do you like strong stuff?" he eventually asked. "It all depends on the standard," I told him, because I assumed he was bluffing. A remarkably obtuse conversation it was.

A few weeks later, he set down on my desk a manuscript that, once he had disappeared from sight, I gave a cursory glance at. What can I say? It appeared to be a promising piece, so I read it through right away. In this short story, which later counted—admittedly only in a very tight circle—as a key work, B. first expounded his fundamental view that Evil was the life principle. The story itself was nevertheless a tale about an ethical deed, or in other words it accounted for the *occurrence of Good*. The story relates that Good can be done in a life in which Evil is the life principle, but only at the cost of the doer's sacrificing his life. It was a daring assertion, just as the prose in which that assertion gained formulation was itself daring. What is more, it all played out within the setting of a Nazi concentration camp.

"Cynical," commented my boss and director, to whose tender consideration I had commended B.'s short story as a "most important work": "the most important work that has passed through my hands in recent years." A more cynical person than he I have never encountered in my life (I mean, doesn't becoming director of a state-owned publishing house, most especially in regard to this particular state, in itself attest to cynicism enough?), and so for that director the word *cynical* was the weightiest weapon in his arsenal of rejection. The story was eventually allowed to see the light of day only in an insignificant publication—to be more precise, a publication that the state had rendered insignificant, appearing semiannually, and then only in a limited run—to which I myself took it. "Is it worth the trouble?" Bee scowled. "Yes, it is," I replied. But I felt something was happening to me; something had begun to ignite within me, as if this whole performance, including the short story itself, had suddenly activated an inner detonator that had, perhaps, been on standby for a long time by then.

Notwithstanding all that, I don't believe I set foot on the path of open rebellion, since I had never been rebellious by nature; at most, my disgust intensified. Admittedly, that disgust did the rest. Anyone who has not lived in a world of undiscoverable reasons; who has never woken up with the very taste of that disgust in his mouth; who has never felt that contagion of general powerlessness spreading throughout his body and gaining mastery over him—that person will not understand what I am talking about. I simply set off on a track—no, not even that: something simply set off with me that, like a train straying over the wrong points, I was no longer able to hold back. I remember a scorching hot summer afternoon that I ought to have been spending digesting a manuscript. It was a matter of a so-called novel, its author's name ranking third or fourth in line, and thus in what was still a very prominent position, within the party hierarchy. In such cases a manuscript is formally circulated, and any editor who receives it for an opinion is well aware what is expected of him, if I may put it that way. As a rule, affairs of this kind are urgent; the book has to be rush-published out of turn. I no doubt had thoughts about literature, editorial integrity, the purpose of my profession, my family (I had a wife and young son by then), but it was not that which was decisive; I sensed from a sudden lurch in my bloodstream that the train had set off with me. I put it in writing that the work's language was atrocious, the structure banal, the story of no interest; I did not recommend publication of the novel. The circulation procedure then had to be reinitiated until two other editors were found to deliver the readers' recommendation that was expected of them. In the meantime the author denounced the publishing house for dilatoriness, mobilized his supporters "at the top," while I myself passed on to another subgroup of humanity, the sort that cannot be trusted.

There is no point in my describing the stations of my

Calvary, as it were, which these days has degenerated into the intellectual's favorite—and well rewarded—pastime. I should not lose sight of the fact that I wish to relate B.'s story (even if merely to salvage my own). My position anyway, at least in relation to the prevailing circumstances, was neither unusual nor especially precarious. In the end I was arrested on charges of propaganda against the state and engaging in the production and distribution of illegal periodicals, though they refrained from lodging a formal indictment and, having held me on remand for almost ten days, let me go. I later heard something to the effect that negotiations over a substantial loan to the state lay at the back of it, in that one condition of the international guarantees stipulated the release of all political prisoners.

Me as a political prisoner—how laughable. "If you're a revolutionary, you shouldn't have started a family," my wife reproached me. The misunderstanding, as in a second-rate farce, was complete. How could I have gotten her to understand that, at bottom, I did what I did for sheer kicks: out of disgust, boredom, and intellectual honesty? How could I have cheapened my heroic undertaking, which this way had at least proved justifiable? How could I have confessed that I had not been guided by either conviction or hope but purely by a wish—how shall I put it?—to break the monotony of the daily grind, to acquire some news of my own existence? In truth, the whole thing was just an innocent prank, a kind of acte gratuit, as Gide would call it, that is taken seriously only in humorless societies such as a dictatorship, for which the police view of the world is the sole basic principle. Consequently, I had to hold my tongue, a supercilious smile on my impassive face, like someone unable to share his unassailable arguments with those who are unworthy of the honor.

If I say it was an idiotic situation, that would not begin to describe its true wretchedness. For my ordinary misdeeds there was an inordinate price to pay: my wife left me, I lost my young son, my job, and my apartment. All of which I formulated at the time as my life fell apart; yet I well remember the indifference, startling even to myself, with which I listened to my wife's incidentally fully justified reproaches, an indifference behind which must have lain more than just my ten-day taste of prison. Would it be odd of me to say that in the very midst of this collapse the feeling I had was more one of relief? All at once, I crossed over from marriage into truth, and I was seized by a sense of adventure on being at the threshold of new beginnings. As far as I could tell, my wife hated me most on account of the house search—quite understandably, by the way, there was no denying it. Apparently three men took over the apartment, turning out drawers, prying into wardrobes, shifting the furniture around. The poor darling had no idea what they were looking for. One man jostled her, another "accidentally" squeezed her breasts so hard as to bruise them, and our two-year-old boy screamed at the top of his lungs. While I was listening to my wife—I recall it precisely—

my attention was increasingly focused on her upper lip, that harmoniously arched, slightly short upper lip with which I had originally fallen in love, and I mused on what an absurd thing love is after all, that a person's entire frail life is founded on such absurdities. One fine day, we wake up with a stranger in a strange bedroom, I thought to myself, and never again do we find our way back to ourselves: Our impossible life is determined by chance, lust, and the whim of a moment, I thought to myself.

Our son in the meantime has grown up; his ambitious mother steered him toward the computerized future, and during our increasingly sporadic encounters I regretfully conclude that I have little to discuss with a computer expert, even though he may be on the brink of an extraordinary future; and if I'm not mistaken, my son likewise shows a certain reserve toward a father who is living the life of those now redundant intellectuals, as a literary editor in a city where, bit by bit, there is no longer any call for literature, let alone editors . . .

No doubt it was not deliberate, but during the ensuing short and dark days into which I plunged, as if I had stumbled into a trench on stepping out from the front door of the house, I realized all of a sudden that I had been released from prison on Christmas Day. It was awkward, but I couldn't help that. I went from one place to another, met up with one person and another—I can't be more specific. Someone let me know that there was going to be a "big bash" on New Year's Eve, someone wanted a word with me, someone wanted to help me regain my job. I got the address from Kürti, who knew Fenyvessy, who knew Halász, who personally knew the legendary Bornfeld, whose articles occasionally appeared in the *New York Times, Le Monde,* and the *Frankfurter Allgemeine Zeitung.* Bornfeld right then happened to be away in the United States, someone said. I had never previously been invited to a gathering of that kind; I suppose it was thanks to my arrest that I had been able, it seems, to make a name of sorts for myself in those exceedingly finicky circles.

It was foggy that New Year's Eve, the city simultaneously empty and thronged with people, with faces and figures emerging unexpectedly from the murk, suddenly, unpredictably, and inescapably, like destiny. Inanely grinning faces, hidden by shoddy hats or caps, were cavorting about; the cars passing by the sidewalks splattered ice-cold black slush onto people. From time to time someone would blow an enormous crepe-paper-fringed cardboard trumpet by my ear, the screech of which filled me with forebodings, like a nightmarish image of the resurrection, while the occasional firecracker would detonate near my feet. I was supposed to make my way to an address in the city center, a clandestine address so to say, where a bunch of nothing but intellectuals cast in the same mold would be celebrating Polish resistance, the latest samizdat publication, and the New Year that was being ushered in.

Somehow B. unquestionably ended up at the center of the party that New Year's Eve, a role he cannot have sought. Or maybe just this once? How had he found his way there, anyway? What business did he have there, among despairing true believers, resolute positivists, and perennially frustrated reformers? What was he doing there, a person who eschewed action, sneered at dreams, had no faith, denied nothing, desired neither to change anything nor to approve anything? No one ever found out. Gloom reigned inside the apartment as well; in fact, I never managed to gain my bearings in it all night. A series of enormous interconnecting rooms that could not be taken in, due to the teeming mass of people; high ceilings, grimy walls impregnated with tobacco smoke, skimpy furnishings; people eating and drinking everywhere, seated on floors, seated on sofas, seated (or lolling) in every imaginable place. Missing was any sign of a host, hostess, or anyone to look after the guests; the evening had obviously been organized on picnic lines, with everyone bringing along something and someone unpacking the parcels, placing the copious quantities of drinks and scanty eatables on tables, someone opening the door if the doorbell rang. The owner of the flat was a person with whom no one, to the very end, was acquainted; his nameplate was on the door, though he may not even have existed. I recollect an almost completely unfurnished room, the floor of which was covered almost wall to wall by a striking silky, greenish blue carpet that almost seemed to ripple in waves. I even well recall, naturally, that I had a lot to drink that night (I had good reason) and so had a hard time making out the rules of a curious game that a smaller circle of the company—Kürti and B. among them—were playing, and with ever-escalating noise and tempers at that.

That too was cleared up a good deal later, after Bee's death, that morning in the publishing house.

"You must be thinking of *Lager* poker," Obláth enlightened me. "A simple game, simple rules. The players sit around the table and each person says *where they have been*. Only the place-name, nothing else. That was the basis for determining the value of the chips. As best I remember, two Kistarcsas were worth one Fő Street . . . one Mauthausen, one and a half Recsks . . ."

"That's open to dispute, though." Kürti showed signs of life. "Even now I would find it hard to decide."

Sarah: "A cynical game, that."

"What was cynical about it?" Kürti flared up. "We had no money, we were only able to play with the values that life had dealt us."

"Am I right in recollecting that Bee pulled out of that hand?" I asked.

"Right." Obláth grinned. "He didn't want to cheat. He must have been aware from the beginning that he had a royal flush up his sleeve."

"Auschwitz." Kürti nodded. "Untrumpable."

I recollect that what followed was a discussion over a modish book title of the time, in which there was a sentence that had become modish at the time, to wit: "There is no explanation for Auschwitz," with Bee's voice gradually standing out from the discussion in much the way that a solo instrument stands out from the orchestral tutti, and for a good while that voice, agitated, spluttering, sometimes choking with passion, dominated. If only I had not been so drunk! Every now and then, a characteristically lucid, typical sentence got through to me even so, but shorn of context, so I forgot the whole thing. There was a face I was bound to recollect, of course, a young woman's face, her gaze in particular, which was fixed on Bee while he was talking, as if seeking to tap a source within him. I had seen her before as she traversed the broad greenish blue carpet as if she were crossing a sea; tiptoeing over to the table, she then sat down without a word. It was Judit, Bee's wife-to-be.

Around daybreak "a word was had with me," as they say. I didn't know the guy. He told me to go into the publishing house in the New Year as if nothing had happened. I took his advice. After a certain amount of fuss (I had to molder for a while as a so-called external worker), I was taken back as an editor of "Foreign Classics" and other series of that kind, where I could do no more damage to anyone; after all, I had no actual police record. I thereby got to meet Bee again, who as it happened was bringing in his translation of a French novel to me as his editor. I had little to do with him, as the translation did not need to be tinkered with at all. The next thing I knew I was confessing to him that I was in real difficulties with not knowing, after what had happened, to whom I was indebted; I had no idea how I should behave, and in some sense I was afraid of myself, given that I had undergone a highly distressing experience in prison.

We had gone down to the café opposite. To my greatest surprise, not only did I relate everything to him without inhibition, it was even gratifying to be able to relate everything to him without inhibition. What I had counted on happening in principle had indeed happened during my first interrogation. I was led into a room where a well-dressed gentleman posed a few questions, shaking his head a lot. I had been a damn fool to do what I did, he said, but nothing worse; indeed, under certain conditions, they would even be prepared to let me go straightaway. As I said, I knew what was going to come next. I won't deny that in one sense I was a bit nervous, but in another, completely calm. However craftily he may have formulated his proposal (even if my life depended on it, I would be unable to recollect what words he used), I understood what he was after, and I unhesitatingly and disdainfully rejected the notion of becoming an informer. We bandied words about for a while longer: there was no need to make such a big deal out of it straightaway, was essentially what he told me, for all it would involve was an occasional conversation, or they might sometimes ask me for a brief written summary, and so on. He was so obsequious that I felt my stubborn and unreasonable resistance was totally idiotic. Whether it was quite by chance that a second man should have come in at this juncture, one who not only was less obsequious than the previous one but paid me not the slightest heed, I have no way of knowing. In lowered voices, they spoke to each other about something for a fair time, and as I was standing there I felt my courage slowly draining away. To put it euphemistically, never in my life had I felt so alone, so destitute. They glanced at me from time to time, now one, now the other, and I distinctly recall an ominous moment when the alarming thought struck me that my interrogators were in course of agreeing they were going to beat me up, or going to summon the specialists into the room in order to have me beaten up. That is not what ensued, fortunately, but the experience of that moment was sufficient to fundamentally shake my self-confidence. Not to put too fine a point on it, I was obliged to admit to myself that if they were to beat me, but more particularly if they were to offer the alternative of either being beaten or signing the piece of paper, it was more than likely that I would have opted to sign. Not absolutely certain, but more likely than not—that's how I felt. Indeed, I was also quite sure that if I were to sign the piece of paper—under physical duress, naturally—I would be able to explain that to myself in just the same way as the variant, naturally more agreeable, in which I did not sign, and—how can I put it?—living with that uncertainty was no easy matter. I struggled with critical philosophical issues in a self-imposed solitary confinement: I am no great believer in metaphysical powers, that's for sure, but ethical categories suddenly seemed to me to be rocky in the extreme. I was forced to an acknowledgment of the stark fact that man is, both physically and morally, an utterly vulnerable being—not an easy thing to accept in a society whose ideals and practice are determined solely by a police view of the world from which there is no escape and where no explanation of any kind is satisfactory, not even if those alternatives are set before me by external duress rather than by myself, so that I actually have nothing to do with what I do or what is done with me.

I don't know why I told him all that, as I was not expecting any advice or assistance from him, and he was aware of that. He heard me out with head bowed, an arm resting on the back of the seat next to him, hand dangling free. From time to time he gave a nod. He looked sad, as if he were already familiar with my case even before I had told him anything, and had long ago drawn some general conclusion from it.

"You shouldn't allow yourself to get into situations like that; you shouldn't allow yourself to know who you are," he said. I suppose I shall never forget that conversation. We are living in an age of disaster; each of us is a carrier of the disaster, so there is a need for a particular art of living for us to survive. Disaster man has no fate, no qualities, no character. His horrific social milieu—the state, dictatorship, call it what you will—tugs on him with the tractive force of a colossal whirlpool, until he gives up his resistance and chaos bursts in on him like a boiling-hot geyser, after which chaos becomes home to him. For him there can be no return to some center of the Self, a solid and irrefutable self-certainty; in other words, he is *lost,* in the most authentic sense of the word.

This being without Self is the disaster, the true Evil, said Bee, though, comically enough, without your being evil yourself, albeit capable of any evil act. A new validity has been gained by the biblical injunction not to be led into temptation, and beware of knowing thyself, else thou shalt be damned, he said.

I don't know why I found so much consolation in these abstract, impersonal thoughts, which I was not even fully able to follow. But it was precisely their generality that I found gratifying, the fact that we were not grubbing around in my case, not analyzing my own psyche: it was precisely this that helped me distance myself from my unconscionably tedious practical concerns, for which there was no solution anyway and which in any case always resolve themselves, just as they resolved themselves on this occasion. On the other hand, all at once, my own case presented itself to me as a theoretical problem, and that was in part fruitful, while in part it also slightly liberated me from myself, which was precisely what I needed then. I told him as much too. I also told him that I felt our conversation had set my incidentally entirely serious deliberations about suicide in a new light: I could say, I said, that I felt it was superfluous for me to weary both myself and society with that. He laughed. He could laugh uproariously, fit to burst. I miss his laughter.

It appears that at one point he contemplated setting the stage piece that he left behind as free verse, in the manner of Peter Weiss or, better still, Thomas Bernhard, being a past master as translator of both. Several of those attempts have survived in the autograph manuscript, among the notes. Also to be found in these are several scenes that, in the end, did not find their way into the play. The characters in one such scene are called Kingbitter and Bee, the scene "a table tucked away at the back of a café."

BEE:

Dying is easy
life is one enormous concentration camp
that God has established here on Earth for mankind
and that man has refined yet further
as an annihilation camp for his own kith
Taking one's own life amounts to
outwitting those who stand on guard
escaping deserting those who are left behind
laughing up one's sleeve
In this big Lager of life
the neither-in-nor-out neither-forward-nor-back
in this wretched world of lives held
in suspended animation where we grow decrepit
without time moving any further forward . . .
this is where I learned that to rebel is
TO STAY ALIVE
The great insubordination is
for us to live our lives to the end
and equally the big humiliation
that we owe ourselves

The sole method of suicide that is worthy
of respect is to live
to commit suicide amounts
to continuing life
starting anew every day
living anew every day
dying anew every day
I don't know how I should continue.

B.'s funeral took place on a bleak, dark autumn day.

No.

I have to go back to the zero setting, if I may put it that way, to the four of us sitting in the publishing house, Sarah, Kürti, Obláth, and me. I made a point of remarking to Sarah out loud that I had managed to get hold of the dictionary she had asked me for the previous week; she immediately took the hint that I wanted a word with her, since she had never asked me for any kind of dictionary, and jumped to her feet straightaway. While we rummaged around among the books by the bookshelf, somewhat away from the others, I quietly asked Sarah what was behind Kürti's unaccustomed irritability. Had he found out anything? Or had Sarah maybe spilled the beans to him? No, said Sarah, they had not spoken about anything of the kind. For quite some time they had not spoken about anything at all. Still, she was not prepared to hide her grief. Unless Kürti had turned completely blind, blind to everything and everyone, he had to suspect something, but she did not think that had caused him any pain. She did not think she was able inflict any pain on him anyway. He's sulking, that's all, said Sarah; and that petulance fitted nicely into the world order of petulance and disillusionment that Kürti had elaborated for himself; Kürti was enjoying all this rather than being hurt by it—at least that was her opinion. He had left the world and his wife equally in the lurch; he no longer had any ties of responsibility to either. He's just like a kid, an adolescent, said Sarah. Yet I did not see her features soften or adopt a more forgiving expression as she was comparing him to an adolescent.

I still don't know how I should continue. There are a few facts that I still find hard to believe, even today, even in retrospect; there are also a few facts that I still find hard to talk about, even today, even in retrospect.

One morning the telephone rang. It must have been nine o'clock (that is overdramatic but no more than the truth). I was still asleep. Around that time I had gotten into the habit of sleeping late because I had started to see that this was the only sensible way I could kill time. It took me a while to grasp that it was Sarah calling: I barely recognized her voice, it was somehow blurred, tormented, and strange. So I immediately asked her if she was in trouble. Big trouble, said Sarah. "I'll be there in a quarter of an hour," I said. "Where?" she said. "Your place, of course," I said, because I supposed something had happened to Kürti. "Come to Bee's!" said Sarah. I was lost for words. "Bee's? You're at his place?" I asked. "Yes, there," she answered. "Can't you pass the receiver to him?" "No," she said. "Why not?" "He's dead," she responded. That was how the conversation went, I swear, like one of Ionescu's macabre dialogues.

I didn't understand a thing. Besides which Sarah was giving a stream of instructions, sobbing maybe, but increasingly intimate in tone: it seemed it must have been a major decision on her part to phone me, and now that she had done so, she was gradually feeling more relieved. I, on the other hand, listened with growing incomprehension: I still did not understand how she had come to be in Bee's apartment, and I was embarrassed by her being so intimate with me, since until that moment I had been acquainted with her only in the way that one is acquainted with a friend's wife, that is to say not acquainted at all, and that was perfectly fine by me. That she was Bee's lover, his last lover—and one could equally put that the other way around—sounded initially, at least to me, quite incredible. Sarah, to all appearances, struck me as a colorless being, and maybe she herself would never have discovered herself had she not run across B. Their relationship must have been an agonizing, one-sided, almost perversely hopeless, and calamitously belated joy.

A good deal later, when our relationship had become closer, indeed, through the demands that I made on her, almost intimate, I often went with Sarah to one café or another, or we would take a stroll and speak about Bee like two widows. In time, it got to the point that I was able to ask her how they had come together in the first place. The story, at least the way Sarah told it, was simple enough, like a fairy tale, and absurd, like our lives. While out shopping one morning—she had scarcely believed her own eyes—she had glimpsed B. in the midst of the bustling crowd in the Central Market Hall. He was in line before a greengrocer's stall, among mountains of vegetables, potatoes, radishes, beetroots, and heads of cabbage, waiting patiently, hands clasped behind his back, for his turn. Like this, even from behind, he was a curious figure, conspicuously out of place, almost ridiculous, and touching, Sarah related. At that point she had not seen B. for quite a while. She took it into her head to play a trick on him. She sneaked up behind him and suddenly slipped her hand into B.'s open palm. Something then happened that she had never anticipated, said Sarah. Instead of turning around (as Sarah had intended), B. had folded the woman's hand tenderly, like an unexpected secret gift, in his warm, bare hand, and Sarah had felt a sudden thrill of passion from that grip, in the typical literary parlance for that sort of thing.

They had then duly greeted each other and exchanged a few words. What was he buying? Sarah asked. Asparagus. What was he going to do with the asparagus? Cook it in salted water and then, yum-yum, eat it, said B. Did he not like it with bread crumbs in melted butter, then? Most certainly he did, only who was going to make it for him? So they had bought butter, bought asparagus, bought bread crumbs, bought a bottle of wine, then lugged the booty up to B.'s apartment. They had nicely unpacked everything—and ten minutes later they were in bed.

That's how the story went. Very typical of B.—or else not at all typical of B., I don't know which. I rarely saw B. in the final months, those eventful months of political changes so full of hope, which then so swiftly turned to ash. In actual fact, even in the few years prior to that I had only rarely ventured to call on him. There was a specific reason for that, which I shall (no doubt reluctantly) get around to in due course.

Before that, however, I ought to relate what happened that morning. In her distressed voice, as I have said, Sarah furnished me with some surprising instructions. I should take a taxi but get out before reaching the apartment block; I should not ring the outside buzzer, at the entrance to the block, and should take care on entering that no one saw me, if at all possible; but above all, I should hurry, hurry, hurry.

As it was, it took almost an hour for me to pull myself together and for the taxi to plow its way across town in the dense traffic. By that time, B. resided in a distinctly run-down neighborhood, in a so-called prefab tower block, in truth a concrete agglomeration somewhere on the borderline between the Józsefváros and Ferencváros districts, "in the entrails of the city," as he himself was in the habit of calling it. He had landed there through his divorce, and there were plenty of people—myself included at the time, if for maybe slightly idiosyncratic reasons—who could not forgive his ex-wife, Judit, on that account.

What, after all that, awaited me within the house and

its garbage-can stench, in the eighth-floor concrete apartment, by then already unbearably stuffy in the morning sunlight, startled and upset me so much that I remember practically nothing other than that. B. was lying in his bed. He was dead. It suddenly occurred to me that I had never seen a dead person before. As I glimpsed B.'s wrapped-up, motionless body, the familiar face frozen in an unfamiliar grimace, my whole body was shaken by a violent jolt, though it was as if a brutal external force were doing it, with me obliged helplessly to submit. I sensed that I was emitting a strange hiccuping sound—I was sobbing—yet I was simultaneously almost amazed by that. I rested my head against the cool white-lacquered door to the room as something, that external force, roughly jarred my shoulder.

I recollect those details with painful clarity even to this day. Also that I dashed out to the kitchen, and because I was retching I kept on gulping water, just like that, from the opened tap. In the meantime my glance fell on a shopping bag that was lying on the kitchen table, with the tip of a baguette and the gold-foiled cork of a champagne bottle poking out of it—heralds of another, more convivial reality—and I suddenly had such a craving for the bread (perhaps because I hadn't breakfasted) that I all but tore a crust from it, except that I was stopped from doing so by the presence of Sarah, who, it seems, had followed me into the kitchen. We conversed in a whisper, as if B. were only sleeping in the next room and we were taking care not to awaken him. Sarah was hardly recognizable, her face puffy, steeped to a red-raw sponge from crying. She said that she had arrived at around half past eight; she had opened the door herself, since she had a key to the apartment. She had rushed first to the kitchen in order to put the shopping down, and only then opened the door to the other room.

Was he already dead then?

Yes.

Did you check?

Leave it!

But . . . but . . . Didn't he write a farewell note?

You saw it yourself.

Indeed I had seen it, only in my shock it had more or less slipped my mind. There it lay in the room, on the table, scrawled on the middle of an A4 sheet of paper:

FORGIVE ME! GOOD NIGHT!

Great big letters they were, but incontestably in B.'s handwriting. Sarah reckoned he must have taken something.

I only wish I knew what. There isn't even a glass of water on the bedside table.

And . . . before that . . . you didn't notice anything about him? Did he not say anything that . . . ?

No, said Sarah.

Admittedly, she had not seen him for two days beforehand.

He had telephoned the evening before, however. He said he had been working hard, he was tired and was about to turn in; he no longer felt like having any supper, but would Sarah bring him breakfast the next day?

"So I brought it. Until now we had never met in the morning."

The conversation could not continue for a while now, with Sarah rocking back and forth in her anguish, then clinging to me while I involuntarily held her to me. There was no trace of the erotic in the gesture, but something stirred within me all the same, I recall. I was base enough (or maybe just male enough? curious enough?) to find an opportunity later on, even amid all the grieving and great panic, to appraise Sarah with a swift, near-reflex glance in a way I had never done before. The moment was undoubtedly unpropitious; Sarah was showing all the signs of breaking down. Still, as I held her in my arms, I did feel that I was holding a *woman* in my arms, an agitated woman, trembling with emotion right now, who was probably hiding interesting secrets. As best I knew, she was of roughly the same age as I, so Sarah too would have been close to mid-forties at the time.

She would never get over this moment of horror, she whispered. B.'s nasty plan of bequeathing his death to her, so to say, and "so undeservedly" into the bargain, would probably make her dislike B. forever, and that was perhaps even more painful for her than any grief, said Sarah.

That had not even occurred to me, to be sure. My glance again alighted on the bottle of champagne, and I pictured Sarah's excitement and anticipation in slipping away from Kürti in order to throw an unwonted love feast for Bee that morning. The moment when she had found Bee dead, though, was too much to bear thinking about. How could he have done that to a woman who loved him? B. was cruel, but not with people—at least not intentionally, and certainly not in a premeditated way.

But then, what else could he have done? After all, he could not have informed Sarah of his plan in advance. Nor would he have wished to be found by pure accident, or that it should be the police who were the first to enter the apartment, for then Sarah would not even have been able to take leave of him. Somehow I had a hunch that B. had probably counted on Sarah calling me for help. One more thought that finally struck me, seemingly almost perverse yet all the same not totally foreign to B., was that he had been able to bank on Sarah bringing some champagne, and had maybe even wanted us to drink a glass there, by his bed. I imparted all that to Sarah. She listened, head bowed, the palms of her hands resting on the kitchen table. I finally added, and immediately regretted doing so, that B. may have wanted Sarah to forget him as soon as possible, probably intending his apparent callousness as an aid.

If he really had thought that way, Sarah snapped straight back, then B. either did not know her or he did not love her, and on the latter score she had never entertained any illusions, she added.

I felt sorry for Sarah, heavy of heart. I felt sorry for myself too, and sorry for B.; I felt sorry for our lives, the now meaningless, untellable lives that were strewn about there in the apartment, as if mowed down by machine-gun-toting thugs.

We said nothing.

But then we had to agree hastily on what next, the urgent practicalities, so to say, of what needed to be done. At that time, Sarah still considered it extraordinarily important that Kürti know nothing. Kürti had to be spared; she reiterated that many times over. She handed me the key that B. had given her. What was suggested first was that Sarah would leave straightaway, while I would wait another half hour before reporting the death officially. I instantly rejected that, however, as—fortunately—I had retained enough presence of mind to think of the manuscripts before all else. I wanted to salvage at least the bulk of the manuscripts before any officials arrived, because once representatives of the authorities had turned up they could sequester the lot. We therefore decided that I would stay in the apartment and save whatever was salvageable, then I would return that afternoon to enter the apartment with the key Sarah had given me, kicking up as much noise as possible in doing so, and only then would I report the death officially, so to say. Sarah then left, though not before taking great care to check that the stairway was deserted. For my part, I searched in a lather and with growing desperation through all the cupboards, drawers, and every imaginable place, as I could not find the novel, or rather manuscript of the novel, that I guessed B. must have written before his death.

As it was, I had to make do with what I found. That in itself was not trifling, but there was this veritable yawning gap: everything in those literary remains cried out for that novel, the fulfillment, the apotheosis.

On a quick reckoning, I managed to pull together material for at least three future volumes, as follows: Apart from the short story that had already been published in the magazine, there were two further stories or novella-length pieces, already known to me, that, due to his dread of the whole process, B. had refused to publish, even though—without wishing to anticipate critical opinion—they were, at least in part, masterpieces of prose. I also found a miscellany of writings that would run to a slim volume: various jottings, aphorisms if you like, each sentence targeted like a shot in the back of the neck, I realized at the time with an editorial jubilation that, alas, had already started to be slowly extinguished within me. The comedy (tragedy?) with the title *Liquidation,* set in 1990, had probably been completed by B. directly before his suicide. The novel, however, of which, as I say, I found not the least trace, had most likely, I surmised, been written by B. before he started on the play, or had possibly been written in parallel with it. It could be he had worked on it for several years, in the same way as he may well have spent a long time—or had there been breaks?—writing the play itself, the evidence for that being the number of variants in form that it underwent, as could be traced through the handwritten notes.

Fortunately, I had my briefcase with me. The briefcase, the battered and worn editor's briefcase that at one time I always carried with me wherever I went, like a physician with his instruments.

Before leaving the apartment, I read B.'s farewell letter one more time:

FORGIVE ME! GOOD NIGHT!

The shortest farewell letter in literary history; a masterpiece in its own right, I thought to myself.

I don't know why, but it now suddenly occurs to me that I did not take another look at the corpse, or, to be more precise, my deceased friend's face. Should I have? I don't know. I simply didn't think of it.

I RECOLLECT PRECISELY THE TIGHT, HEAVY SENSAtion in my chest as I suddenly awoke that night. Surely not a heart attack? I thought to myself, with a touch of inner glee. It wasn't. On the other hand, all at once I felt utterly stupid and cheated, as if I had been outwitted and deceived with childish ease. Someone had lied to me, and—odd as it may sound—that someone had been mostly myself. I posed myself a few questions that I ought to have posed much earlier, even right away, there, on the spot. Had I, for instance, given any thought to B.'s motives, the real reason or reasons for his fateful act? That old stuffy café in which we had talked about suicide came back to mind. Why had I accepted B.'s suicide so lightly, indeed with such equanimity? Literature must have been to blame, nothing else; literature, which had so leached the life out of me that life's natural logic no longer even impinged on my way of thinking. After all, a person does not surrender his life so lightly. I had an intimation of some sort of secret; a hazy backdrop had intruded itself behind events that I myself, despite being a participant in those events, had failed to notice at the time. True, I had seen the dead body, and that had in some sense paralyzed me. From that moment on, I had regarded anything as being possible, including the farewell letter that was thrust under my nose. Now, in the dark room, on my back in bed, I suddenly mused with shame that I had accepted—indeed, to myself called a masterpiece—a provocatively impossible nonsense scrawled on a scrap of paper that would be unworthy not only of B. but of any mature adult. Why had they done that to me? I cogitated. How was it possible for B. to summon Sarah, his lover, to a champagne breakfast and leave her a farewell note like that? No, it wasn't possible; it was perfectly obvious that it wasn't. It suddenly occurred to me that maybe two farewell letters existed, a genuine one and, well, the one intended for my eyes. But what had any of that to do with the vanished novel—for by then I was already considering it, very self-assured, as "the vanished novel"—the mystery of which, so I sensed, was likewise to be sought here?

I was unable to come up with answers to any of the questions. I set about preparing the material that was in my hands for publication, as they say, telling Sarah that she would have to assist me in editing B.'s literary estate. That is how our secret meetings began, the lengthy conversations and walks during which I allowed Sarah to give free rein to her grief. At times she seemed utterly lost, and I was horrified to find myself thinking that, if I really wanted, maybe I could pick up where Bee had left off. That notion filled me with shame and uneasiness, because it conjured up a past about which it was not permissible for me to speak, let alone know.

It was its impossibility that made our relationship so wonderful, said Sarah.

"It was so wonderful, so unreal," Sarah recounted, "like a dream." Unburdened by any genuine cares. They had met and gone for walks like adolescents, shared their "otherworldly secrets" with each other, was how Sarah put it. They had talked about despair, about books and music, sometimes about Judit. Sarah was convinced that B. was still in love with Judit. I didn't press her further about that; quite the contrary, I steered well clear of it. Indeed, if I were to be frank, I could even say that I beat a hasty retreat from posing any further questions relating to Judit. As it was, though, that fact did not bother Sarah; she had accepted it, she said, just as she had accepted their relationship. It had happened to be right around the time that Kürti began to find himself at odds with the world, she said. I asked her how that had manifested itself. Most of all in interminable harangues, said Sarah. He would start in the morning and finish in the evening.

They had been moralizing harangues, in the course of which, each and every time, Kürti would expound over and over again how a thing was not the way it should be, and why the thing was not the way it should be. The harangues were monotonous, unbearable, and usually culminated in grotesque, scary fits of rage. Should Sarah interrupt in order to head off the fit of rage, however, he would fly into a fit of rage anyway. The story devastated me, because it was the story of my onetime friend, and moreover it patently revealed what a life built on groundless hopes led to. Kürti had believed in politics, and politics had deceived him, the way politics deceives everyone.

I SEE NO POINT IN GIVING A DETAILED DESCRIPTION of the struggle I engaged in with Sarah until victory, unexpected and by then no longer hoped for, finally fell into my lap like an overripe fruit. I can't say I was overjoyed; there are times when one would prefer not to be right.

It struck me that I was practically unable to speak to her at all about B.'s work. I asked her if she knew what B. had been working on during the months before his death; she didn't know. But she didn't believe, she said, that he was entertaining any plans for a more substantial piece of writing, except that he wanted to make a new translation of *The Radetzky March,* the current translation of which he took a dim view of. I just stared in disbelief at her, thinking that anger at the terrible humiliation Sarah had suffered at B.'s hands was still at work. If I considered her sense of loss, what kind of emotional abyss she had sunk into on B.'s death, I needed to understand that during that period nothing else could have been of interest to her. Later on, as I gradually got closer to her, I was startled to discover that Sarah was a deeply religious soul who regarded life as a duty, and for her Kürti embodied that duty. For all that, despite Kürti and despite her relationship with B., which had been fragile and had to be nursed like a rose in winter (as Sarah herself put it), she had been unable to stand aside from the high tide of general euphoria around her, the general climate of great hopes and great relief. She had gone to Heroes' Square, taking a candle and lighting it, standing with it in the crowd until night had drawn in, and she had sung along with the crowd in the lights of those tens of thousands of candles. None of that had been of any interest to B.; Kürti had been simply angered by it all. Sarah understood neither of them; this once she was able to share her joy only with the crowd. On this matter something had separated her from Bee, and that, said Sarah, had been an untouchable, insoluble, indeed at times frightening issue.

I didn't understand exactly what she was talking about.

Bee was Jewish, said Sarah.

But we know about that, I rejoined.

"We don't," said Sarah. "We don't know what it means to be Jewish." She hesitated a little before suddenly declaring that I ought not to get so preoccupied with Bee's literary estate.

I was astounded. "What do you mean by that?"

"It would be best to leave everything as it is, in manuscript," said Sarah. The alarming thought suddenly struck me that maybe B. had willed the copyright to her; I even asked her as much. Sarah said nothing for a long while, and it doesn't matter what I read from her face; it was perfectly clear that at that moment I was not in her good books. Yet she then said she probably ought to let me in on something, even though it concerned her alone. It concerned a piece of writing, or, more specifically, a document, she added.

My heart skipped a beat, as the expression goes.

"A letter?" I asked.

"Yes," she replied.

By the next day, though, she had had second thoughts.

In the end, she brought herself to show me after all.

We met in a coffeehouse. I could read it there but was not allowed to take it away; that was the condition. In the end, she consented to my copying it in my own hand, there at the table, onto a piece of paper, as if photocopiers or computers had not yet been invented.

It was a farewell letter, the farewell letter Bee had written to Sarah that she had not shown me there, in the apartment, and was showing me now only in order to dissuade me from my plans and enjoin me to silence: that was what her conscience dictated.

Sarah, this is the end. The end. I am aware of the wrong I am doing you, but this is the end. The end.

I may be writing these lines in a morphine rush, but I am in possession of my faculties. I have never been as lucid as this. I am practically radiating light, my own lantern.

Don't think I have no regrets. An end to those long afternoons of ours that melted into the murk of evening. An end to those "otherworldly caresses" (that's what we called them, remember?). We lay in bed like two siblings, little sister and big brother—no, more like two gentle sisters cosseting each other. An end to our world, this—I see it now—cozy prison world that we so loathed. Yet that loathing kept me alive, I know that now. Defiance, the defiance to survive.

"And what about love?" you would ask. I can hear your voice. "Doesn't love count?"

I don't know, Sarah. You did all you could. I'm sorry.

I have to vanish from here, along with everything that I carry within me—how can I put it?—like a plague. I am carrying incredible destructive forces within me; it would be possible to destroy the entire world with my resentment, to put it nicely and not say anything nauseating.

For a long time, all I have wished for is my own destruction. But that won't happen of its own accord; I have to lend a hand, give it a push . . .

I have brought into existence a creation, a delicate,

fragile life, simply in order to destroy it. If you know anything, keep it quiet. I am like god, that scoundrel . . .

I yearn for my destruction with all my heart. I don't know for what reason I have had to keep on with this long life, although I could have been murdered before it was too late, when I was still unacquainted with ambition and the futility of struggle. There was no sense in any of it; I have not managed to bring anything into existence; the sole product of my life is that I have been able to gain acquaintance with the sense of strangeness that separates me from life. I was already dead while I was living. You embraced a dead man, Sarah, and your attempts to reanimate him were in vain. There were times when I viewed us from afar, your futile efforts, and I was barely able to bottle up the laughter that was aching to get out. I'm a rotten person, Sarah.

You were a great consolation in this wretched, this worldly Lager *that is called life, Sarah.*

Don't feel sorry for me; I had a perfect life. Of its kind. All one has to do is recognize, and that recognition was my life. But now it is the end. The pretext for my existence has ceased; the existential condition of surviving has ceased. I ought now to live like an adult, like a man. But I have no inclination for that, no inclination to step out of the prison into infinite space to watch the dwindling and evaporation of my superfluous . . .

Surely I wasn't about to say "tragedy"!

How ridiculous.

I loved the inexhaustible green of plant life; I loved water; I loved swimming; and until I met her, I thought I also loved women.

I experienced everything that was there to be experienced by me. I was almost killed, and almost became a killer myself. Or rather . . . well, I am preparing to kill right now.

You have seen me bowed over piles of paper. If you know anything, keep it quiet. Our man of letters is going to pump you. I tried to formulate the . . . It doesn't matter. It was no good. There is nothing, nothing at all. I left nothing for him. There's nothing worth the mention. I have no wish to pitch my stall in the literary flea market; shoddy goods, not fit to place in human hands. Then again, I have no wish to be picked up, prodded, and then tossed back. I have finished what I have to do, and that is no one else's business.

I am starting to feel odd. It's so good that I am through with it . . . so good to dump everything. I no longer have anything to do with the pile of atrocious and revolting stuff that is me . . . Thanks for everything . . . Thanks for the dream . . .

That was the letter, then. Word for word. I don't think I grasped it at all on the initial reading. All I felt was a sense of triumph, the dubious triumphalism of being right. I perceived in it, in sum, proof of all I had suspected. There was the novel—or rather not there, exactly, but indubitable signs of his having written it, that the novel did indeed exist, that its existence was a fact and an indisputable reality. The only puzzle was the last sentence. *Thanks for the dream.* What did he mean by the word *dream?* Could he have been thinking of Calderón, of whom he was so fond, especially his play *Life Is a Dream? "El delito mayor del hombre es haber nacido"*—man's greatest crime is to be born. How many, many times I heard him quote that sentence, coined so long before Schopenhauer's time.

A bit odd, to be sure, but that was what I was thinking. The degenerate way of thinking, I concede, of a literary editor who is capable of interpreting even the most obvious facts of life only by mobilizing the resources of world literature. Let me plead in mitigation that at the same time this way of thinking did also spare me—at least for a short while—a certain amount of anguish, from having to sustain the full weight of the reality of my poor friend's ghastly thoughts and appalling end. This self-defense, my protest against reality, even went to the point that it occurred to me to question the letter's authenticity. The text suggests a total spontaneity of formulation: at its end the pen all but falls from B.'s grasp. Could that be accepted? It is no easy matter, in truth, to assess the difference between stylization and reality, especially if one's dealing with a writer, I thought to myself; they stylize themselves to the point that in the end, as the adage goes, the style is the man.

But the question as to whether the letter was, ultimately, a fiction that merely mimicked exhaustion, the gradual extinction of life, was truly dwarfed by the other question: if it was not a matter of Calderón-type reminiscence, then why did he thank Sarah for the dream? More specifically, why did he thank *Sarah* in particular for the dream? According to his words, *Morpheus already had him in his arms;* two women were sculling with him on the black river, the other, without any doubt, going by the name of Judit . . .

Could he possibly have been thanking Judit for the dream? A chill ran down my spine . . . I was reminded of the policeman. It occurred to me that Bee had occasionally paid visits to Judit in her clinic, sometimes asking her for prescriptions—that much I knew from Bee himself. Suddenly it became evident to me that the vanished novel must somehow be connected with Judit. But how?

Up to this point, these had all been no more than thoughts, cold-blooded thoughts. But now I suddenly realized that I had to speak with Judit. I had to call her up, meet with her. As I reached for the telephone, however, I felt the blood quite literally drain from my hand and my feet.

I had not seen her for some five years. Though now that I thought about it, she had been at the funeral. She had arrived late and stood a little way off from us, her former friends. She was holding two children by the hand, a little boy and a little girl, and she had left before the ceremony was concluded. I had tried to forget about her, without success. She was a bit plumper than she had been of old, self-assured and unapproachable. For two days after the funeral, I was tormented by practically incessant masturbatory spasms. It was like some mischievous, wicked metaphysical punishment for the several-months-long love affair that I had conducted back in the past with my master and great friend's wife.

I have no wish to speak about that affair. I couldn't, even if I wanted to. I don't even know exactly what it was, what name I could devise for it. Sexual passion—well, yes, but shot through, at least on my part, with fear, disgust, self-loathing, and inexplicable delights. I got to know all of Judit's unashamed secrets, while she herself became an ever-greater secret to me. In the end, I was afraid of her in the same way that I was also afraid of myself.

I knew that since then she had remarried, lived in a villa in Buda, and her husband was an architect. She withdrew from our circle, so to say. I don't wish to know what I think about that. Once, later on, when—in the interests of the novel, purely the vanished novel—I felt that I would have to resort to hard, if not actually callous, tactics against her, I asked Sarah for her assistance.

"What are you *really* after?" Sarah asked. "To avenge yourself on the victors?"

Her question startled me, but my answer startled me even more. I remember it exactly because the answer registered with me as if I were the listener, so to say, as if it were not I but someone else who was speaking.

"She can't step out of the past as easily as she imagines. Fresh and fragrant, like out of a bathtub of dirty water."

I then launched into prolonged explanations, trying to convince Sarah (myself too, perhaps) that I had not said what I had said. Sarah's response was that grief and the loss had not hardened her as it had me, so it appeared. She added, moreover, that instead of jealousy, what she felt nowadays was more a kind of (she had difficulty finding the right word) "sisterhood" toward Judit. But then she immediately added that, in all likelihood, I would not understand, indeed was incapable of understanding, in the way that men in general were not much given to understanding that sort of thing; that it was easier to hate than to love, and love for losers was hate.

I did not reply, which I myself found odd.

I'M AFRAID I AM UNABLE TO GRAPPLE WITH WHAT should come—or does or did come—next. I lack something, the testimony of the eternally impassive eye, if I may put it in such a way. For I have observed that with writers, true writers I mean (and I cannot deny here that I have met only one true writer, Bee), the eye impartially and incorruptibly registers even the emotionally or physically most testing events, while the rest of the mundane personality, if I may put it in such a way, becomes completely integrated into those events in exactly the same way as happens with anyone else. I would go so far as to declare that literary talent may, at least partly, be no more than this impassive eye, this state of strangeness that can subsequently be coaxed into speech. It is a half step, a distancing of half a pace, whereas I always progress together with things, always pervaded by events, always disturbed by and buried under the facts.

In short, I called Judit up at the clinic where she worked as a dermatologist. She was none too cordial; I would go as far as to say she did not even bother to listen. The next time she ordered the nurse to take the call. The nurse said the consultant was right in the middle of examining a patient. Nothing to the effect that I should call again later. I didn't try either, but I did call her at home, at a time when, to the best of my knowledge, your average citizen is sitting down to supper. A pleasant male voice answered. I gave my name and asked if I might speak to the consultant. I even heard the distant male voice: "Judit! One of your patients!" Followed by Judit. An irritated yet perhaps slightly apprehensive tone: "What is so urgent that it can't wait until tomorrow? All right, see me at the clinic then." I was cheeky enough to ask her what her clinic hours were. "In the afternoon. Between three and eight," she said, rather angrily too, I felt. I remember being extraordinarily pleased with myself. When I put the receiver down, there's no denying, I murmured "Smarty-pants!" under my breath.

Then I didn't call for two days. Let her stew, or something like that, I thought to myself. This time she was more responsive than before, albeit still very reproachful. What in fact did I want from her? I would like to speak with her, I said. She already knew that, but what did I want to speak about? She would see, I said. And she would be very grateful if I didn't call her at home, all right? I would not have called if she hadn't raised her hackles from the start, I said. I suggested we meet in a café. She rejected that out of hand. She rejected all my suggestions. I should come in to the clinic. That was rejected by me. I had definite ideas about our encounter. I saw myself meeting her on the terrace of a Danube-bank coffeehouse. It was spring. I wanted to see her walking briskly toward me in a spring dress. As it turned out, she did not come from the direction I had been expecting but arrived suddenly, so by the time I spotted her she was already standing at the table.

Tiny goofs and blunders like that are a necessary part of life. In some sense they validate a person; the very fact that a human is human, and nothing ever works out the way it should.

Awkward minutes ensued, banal exchanges. I recall that in response to some question from Judit I said, with a shabby, bogus smirk: "I just wanted to see you."

"You had a chance not long ago," Judit rejoined.

"Not long ago? When?"

"At the funeral."

A frightful dialogue. Now that I am writing it down, only now do I see how frightful. The cemetery suddenly appeared before my eyes. A dank, blustery afternoon. Ragged clouds racing across the sky, sporadic wintry showers. There are few people. No one speaks. A stark, secular ceremony without a eulogy. Who had wanted that? Who had made the arrangements? Odd, but I don't know. How could we not have spoken about it? About a fitting funeral for B. How come it hadn't entered any of our heads? I recall I was looking at Sarah. She was sobbing, incapacitated, laid bare, her anguish, like an illness, having totally gotten the better of her. Obláth with his bowed head, hands locked in front of his raincoat, Kürti staring straight ahead with a vacant look in his eyes. Two men in black uniforms hastily stowed the urn in the back of a black hearse. A doubt as to whether anybody had given them a tip crossed my mind. At this moment, with hurried steps, the two children in tow, Judit comes into sight among the gravestones. They come to a stop some distance away. I did not dare look over there. The hearse sets off. The procession sets off. In the end, I have no idea whether Judit joins us or not. I didn't see her at the cinerarium (which doesn't necessarily mean she was not there).

Fortunately, a waitress appeared. Judit did not want to order anything.

"There's no point," she said. "Believe me, there is no point in this." She tensed as if about to stand but did not get up. The waitress did not move either. I suggested a coffee. She shrugged. All at once, I caught myself launching into a stream of fatuous reproaches: "You took great care that no one should disturb your solitary mourning. You stood apart from us all, there, in a black suit, holding a little girl with one hand, a little boy with the other . . ."

"My children," said Judit. She had had to bring them

from the nursery. "You can't ask me to lock the poor little things in the car like two puppies," she said.

"Your old friends were there. Obláth, Kürti, Sarah, me, the others . . . You didn't have so much as a single word for us," I gripe like a sulky adolescent.

Judit stirs her coffee without saying anything. Then she slowly and coolly raises her eyes to me.

"I'm living a different life now, Kingbitter," she says.

"We're all living different lives."

"Philosophizing as ever," she says irritably. "If you invited me here to tell me something, then get on with it, please . . . I have to go in five minutes."

"I won't detain you. Not for a second. Provided you hand B.'s last novel over to me."

I SENSE THAT I'M SLIGHTLY DEPARTING FROM . . . what indeed? Reality? How could I depart from reality, totally incomprehensible and unknowable as it is, through being eternally shielded from us by our imaginations, thank God! All I would say is that I may, even quite inadvertently, be dramatizing the dialogues, having only hazy recollections of them, and they were no doubt a lot duller and simpler than what is recorded above. In my discomfiture, I may have started by saying straight out that certain circumstances had instilled in me the suspicion that B. had written a novel before he died. The same circumstances led me to suppose that this novel might be in her, Judit's, hands. Insofar as that was the case, it was respectfully requested, et cetera.

Judit is initially disconcerted but then begins to protest vehemently. Novel? She knows nothing about any novel.

"What novel are you talking about, for God's sake!"

"The one he finished before his death. And which he handed to you, either as a manuscript or a typescript."

"I wish I knew where you got that idea. Did he tell you? Or maybe write it down somewhere? In his will, a letter, or . . ."

"Look here, Judit, I may only have been guessing so far, but now I'm sure that the manuscript is with you."

"Really?"

"Why don't you want to give it to me?"

"Simple: because it doesn't exist."

"It has to exist," Kingbitter proclaims, and so certain is he on the matter that he can all but feel the creased manuscript, hear the rustle of the pages as he thumbs through it. From where he draws that great certainty, he himself does not know. So firm is his conviction that he truly drives Judit to despair.

"You're like a private dick in some American crime thriller," she moans. "All this cross-examination. By what right? What leads you to think that a novel about which you know nothing actually exists? And even if it did exist, why would I have it? Doesn't it bother you that we divorced five years ago?"

"That's neither here nor there. I know that he still had a vague sense of guilt toward you. And a sense of guilt is the only true bond between two people."

"I know another kind as well," says Judit.

"Such as?"—and that question may have sounded more provocative than Kingbitter intended. Judit, naturally, does not deign to reply; or rather, her silence is her reply.

"Obviously, you too had some sense of guilt toward him," Kingbitter continues, "otherwise you would not have called him up from time to time."

"How do you know that?"

"From him."

Silence.

"You know there was always something wrong with him. I prescribed him sleeping tablets, tranquilizers, analgesics . . ."

"Nothing else?"

"Else? What else?"

"For example," and at this point Kingbitter hesitates slightly before blurting out, "morphine, for example."

Another silence ensues. The quiet that precedes distressing confessions.

"The cause of death was a morphine overdose," Kingbitter notes, by way of a cue.

"A masterstroke. Don't you despise yourself? I know very well what the cause of death was. But what do you know? You know nothing at all, and how mean you are even in that. To start with, you surely don't imagine I would prescribe morphine for an outpatient in a skin clinic! And for injection into the bargain!"

"Then, dammit, who the hell did he get the morphine from?"

"From me."

"I don't quite follow that," exclaims Kingbitter, taken aback.

"Why would you follow?" says Judit. "You generally don't follow anything. I could have written prescriptions for him in any café; there was no need for him to visit the clinic for that."

"And so?" says an uncomprehending Kingbitter.

"He always wanted to come to the clinic," says Judit. "He sat there among the dermatological cases. It was dreadful. Until I caught on to the reason."

One evening, it seems, on checking through the contents of the drug cabinet after consulting hours were over, Judit had been unpleasantly surprised to discover that the morphine stock had been pilfered from. Quite apart from the need to make up the loss, she was now faced with every clinic doctor's nightmare: a mystery addict who was stealing the necessary daily supply during surgery hours. The key to the drug cabinet is not invariably put in one's pocket: One might open and shut the cabinet but forget the key in the lock. Every doctor is mindful of the lengths to which addicts will go to procure a supply. She looks through the list of patients who had called in that afternoon. B. had dropped in before consulting hours were under way. And it suddenly crossed her mind that she had slipped out of the room for a minute because Bee had urgently needed a pen and she didn't have one on her. The next time, she herself arranged to leave B. on his own in the room. From then on she would make herself available to B. only at appropriate intervals. She would always leave the appropriate dose in the drug cabinet, and it would always vanish from there.

Kingbitter is devastated by the story. He splutters inarticulately, "But that's . . . that's outrageous." Judit's features remain hard. She can think of greater outrages than that, she says.

"Greater than that?" Kingbitter remonstrates. "What?"

"Like having him registered and then leaving him to wait his turn, among the broken-down addicts in the district clinic, to be doled out the dose that the state sees fit. The fix that 'users' are permitted. I don't know how else he would have obtained it."

Kingbitter remains quiet for a bit. What he has heard has shaken him.

"He was a drug addict?"

"That's one way of putting it. He started the habit somewhere at some point. At least this way I could keep him on a short leash, check the doses . . ."

"Why did you say nothing?"

"To whom?"

"To me, for example?"

"And if I'd told you? Would you have packed him off into a compulsory detox program?"

Kingbitter remains silent. He had not anticipated that question.

"Or maybe you'd have gotten him switched over to some other drug?" Judit continues, implacably. "One that was even more harmful?"

Kingbitter remains silent. There you are, Judit continues, the great moralist. The private dick. Now listen up, I'm going to tell you something. If he was capable of skipping fixes solely in order to stash away a big enough dose—if he was capable of that degree of discipline, that degree of abstinence, then that means he was ready for anything. Does Kingbitter understand what that says about him? Because Kingbitter hasn't the least idea what torments Bee would have to go through in the meantime, not a clue what missing a dose means for a junkie.

Both now fall silent.

"So, in your view"—Kingbitter finally speaks—"he prepared for it."

"That's right," answers Judit.

"From a long time back, systematically."

"It had to be that way."

"And you noticed nothing."

"No, because he only ever got just enough to keep him going till the next visit. Actually, less and less, because I put him on a withdrawal course of slowly tapering doses."

They again fall silent for a while.

"What, in fact, do you want to hear from me, Kingbitter?" Judit finally says. "He would still have been able to hoard doses even if he had been getting his supply through official channels . . . Only at what a price in humiliation . . . And another thing, Kingbitter, just to assuage your moral imperatives. You know . . . if I really had seen signs that he was reaching the very end of his tether, and he had asked me how and in what manner . . . If, by any chance, he had turned to me for advice . . . Do you see what I'm driving at? Even then I wouldn't have been able to recommend a better way. It's still the easiest and gentlest . . . And if you happen to be thinking of asking some stupid stuff about whether I have any twinges of guilt, then . . ."

But Judit is unable to finish the sentence. She suddenly crumples, on the face of it illogically and thus all the more surprisingly. She buries her face in her hands and is shaken by sobbing. She must have stuffed something in her mouth, perhaps a handkerchief, from behind which there are bursts of strangled, hiccuping sounds. Kingbitter tries desperately, ineffectually to calm her down.

"Let's get out of here . . . Let's go," says Judit.

They get up. Kingbitter pays for the coffees. He then takes Judit by the arm.

ALL I DID WAS BRING HER HOME. HERE, TO MY place. Perfectly naturally, without any devious ulterior motive. Where else could I have taken her? She came with me, didn't raise a peep. I asked her if there was anything I could do for her. Wouldn't she like to tidy herself, maybe have a drink?

"What?"

"A vodka, say."

She wasn't paying much attention, however, I could see. She was studying the room.

"You still live here," she said. "Nothing has changed. It hasn't even been painted since then, I suppose."

"No. Though it could do with it," I noted in passing. "Have a seat," I urged.

"Here?" she asked, stopping beside a particular armchair. She smiled. To keep my composure, I thought to myself that every place has a particular armchair, or a particular couch; every place has that particular piece of furniture. I asked her again if she wanted anything to drink.

She made herself comfortable on the couch. She deliberated.

"A vodka. Kirsch. Mixed-fruit schnapps," she enumerated, dreamy-faced.

"Glory days." I endeavored to jest. She didn't answer. All of a sudden, she became more congenial, quite human.

"How do you live here, Kingbitter?" she asked. She had always addressed me by my surname, which I used to greatly relish.

"Like a private dick in an American pulp thriller," I tried to quip.

"And how does a private dick live?"

I had to ponder that.

"Privately. Always waiting for the chance."

"What kinds of chance are you waiting for, then?"

"Me? At best, the ones I'm still able to miss."

She laughed.

"Love?" she went on to ask.

"Don't be silly."

"Women?"

"A full-time hooker every now and then. Sometimes a literary groupie. Sometimes both in one."

Once again I started to be overcome by an icy repulsion. Who was I talking to here? About what? It was a repulsive conversation, excruciating, humiliating, intolerable.

"Let's have a drink," I proposed at last. I got to my feet and searched in the cupboard. "I've only got vodka in the house," I announced. Strangely enough, in response to this information her expression suddenly altered, almost, I might say, like someone suddenly sobering up.

"I haven't drunk vodka for a long time now," she said rather morosely.

That prompted me to ask: "What do you drink, then? Champagne?"

"Yes, I do," she replied.

"Preferably branded," I said.

"Dom Pérignon," she concurred. We held our silence for a while.

"This is sneaky, Kingbitter," she started up again. "I see what you're playing at, but you're on the wrong track. My husband is an architect, has a good income, we have a good life. But that's not the essential thing, not at all."

"What, then?" I asked, sensing that desperation and awareness of my loss were getting the better of me.

"I don't know if it's right for me to say it out loud," I heard her voice saying meanwhile. "Here, in this seat."

"Just out with it, Judit. Out with it all."

"I don't know if you'll hate me."

"What if I do? . . . Does it matter?"

"How do I know it's not going to set me at odds with people? With everything, the entire world?"

"Be glad about it. The world is beastly."

"I don't know if . . . all things considered . . . I don't know if it's not a sin."

"You've made me curious now. Spit it out finally, Judit."

She held me in suspense for a few more seconds.

"I'm happy, Kingbitter," she murmured, as if it were some intimate confession, though not one aimed at me. By the time she had finished saying it, I felt annihilated. Everything had been taken away from me, even though I had nothing.

Could it have been that which made me lose my head? All I recall is a hectic jumble, a struggle, body heat. In the palm of one hand a breast, the thumb of the other pressing her clitoris through her underwear. I finally became conscious that nothing was happening; I was holding a lump of wood in my arms, a puppet, a corpse. Only then did I grasp what I was doing.

I let her go.

We said nothing, the way people usually say nothing after something shameful has happened.

I mumbled something by way of an apology.

She said: "I knew I could not utter that word without it having consequences."

Then: "I can't go to bed with you purely out of nostalgia. Or for the sake of the friendship we once had."

Then: "I love my husband. And since I love him, I've also come to like myself."

In the meantime we scrabbled to put our clothes in order, backs half turned to each other. If I remember correctly, I again launched into an apology.

"The old feelings took over completely" is what I said.

She was just in the middle of applying lipstick, holding a small mirror to her face. For a second I had a deceptive feeling we had made love after all. Obviously on account of the lipstick. She had always rouged her lips after a rendezvous.

"What 'old feelings'? If you had to define them more precisely, what would you say?" she asked, making little grimacing pouts in the mirror.

"It was mad. Crazy. But the kind of insane that is still called love," I replied, horrified myself at how empty the words were. All at once, I grasped the absurdity of our situation; the fact that our story, like every story, was incomprehensible and irrevocable, had gone, slipped by, been engulfed, and we no longer had anything to do with it, just as we have hardly anything to do with our lives. It entered my head that only writing can restore this process, the unbrokenness of our lives, and in point of fact the reason we were there was that I might lay hands on B.'s lost novel.

As a result, I heard what she said only as if it were coming from somewhere far away: "You left me high and dry. You signed up to teach at a high school somewhere in the country; you even kept your address a secret."

That was true. It had been the only way I was able to

free myself from the relationship, which had given me so much joy and so much torment. Alarmed to see her hand already on the door latch, I asked her swiftly, almost at random, whether she had been called into the police station.

"Why would they have wanted to see me?" she said in astonishment, taking her hand off the latch. I related the business with the policeman, and said that if they hadn't put in an appearance by now, it was unlikely they would do so at all; there was nothing to fear, since, unless she had told anyone, what she had done could not be proved.

Seeing that put her mind at rest, I then asked her if she could think of any explanation for B.'s suicide.

"He was burnt out," she said after some deliberation, softly and, so it struck me, with deep feeling. "The resistance was gone; the whole world had opened up before his eyes. And by then he was fed up with having to seek out new prisons for himself."

Yes, that sounded right. I asked her whether she had met or spoken with Bee immediately before his death.

Neither, she said.

Then how had the manuscript reached her? I asked.

What manuscript? Back to the novel, were we? Why wouldn't I accept that no novel existed?

Because, I said, it must exist.

Where had that fixed idea come from, and why was I unwilling to let go of it?

Listen here, Judit: a person doesn't die like that. Just about anyone else, yes, but not him. I have the choice of either disbelieving he died or disbelieving that he left something behind. That he died is a fact. Which leaves the other conclusion: that the literary estate is incomplete. Something is missing. The synoptic work, the *book.* He would not have gone without that; you don't impute that kind of dilettantism to a true writer.

Come to your senses, Kingbitter. This is crazy talk.

I don't believe it's nonsense. It is my belief that has kept me going in this career, Judit. What would a publisher's reader be without belief, an intellectual challenge, in a censored, evil, and illiterate world? No one and nothing. A paper-marking slave, a proofreader groping in the dark. But I believe in writing—nothing else; just writing. Man may live like a worm, but he writes like a god. There was a time when that secret was known, but now it has been forgotten; the world is composed of disintegrating fragments, an incoherent dark chaos, sustained by writing alone. If you have a concept of the world, if you have not yet forgotten all that has happened, that *you have a world* at all, it is writing that has created that for you, and ceaselessly goes on creating it; *Logos,* the invisible spider's thread that holds our lives together. There is an ancient, biblical word: *scribe.* It has long fallen out of use. A scribe is something different from a talent, different from a good writer. He is not a philosopher, not a linguist nor a stylist. Even if he stammers, and you don't immediately understand him either, you instantly recognize a scribe. Bee was a scribe. What he left behind cannot be lost, because he left it behind for us. His secret is tucked away in that—not just his secret, but ours as well. Also why he did what he did. And from that, I have to find out whether I must follow him or can choose otherwise. It may be no more than five words that have to be deciphered, but those five words are the teaching. The quintessence, the sense.

Teaching, quintessence—you're starting to scare me, Kingbitter.

With good reason, Judit. You have to hand the manuscript over. I have to read it, edit it, get it out to people. You can't duck the answer, Judit. I'll go to any lengths, even blackmail, if I have to.

With what? How?

I don't know yet, but I'll find a way. I'll talk to your husband.

Don't do that, Kingbitter.

Oho! That got you going.

Don't foul up my life. There's no point, it won't get you anywhere anyway. My home is a long way from . . .

You're not going to dissuade me or change my mind. I'll stop at nothing. I'm capable of anything, Judit.

Yes, I can see that. You're scaring me.

THE REASON I LOVED LIVING WITH YOU, ADAM, IS that you never sought to tear away that shred of strangeness that, it seems, every love needs.

I remember how I waited for you that evening. I laid the table on the terrace, lit candles in the still air of the spring evening. I had already given the children supper and put them to bed. I heard the car not long afterward. It was so quiet I even heard the soft hum of the roller door of the garage as it lifted, then your car, the clunk of the door, your footsteps, and finally, your voice: you called out to me. I hurried to meet you, and the heel of my shoe caught for a moment in some silly chink by the doorsill, almost pitching me over.

I would like to remember that moment even more clearly, because it will never be repeated. It's so odd how love passes. The world suddenly turns gray around you; it becomes cold, comprehensible, sober, and distant.

A man had come to see you, a man named Kingbitter. He claimed to have something extraordinarily important to tell you. He spoke about some curious things. He placed a folder on your desk, then left. There were seventy or eighty closely typed pages of manuscript in the folder; a miscellany of texts, notes, aphorisms. You read it the whole afternoon. It was as if weights had been dropped on you. You are no longer the man you were up till then, nor am I any longer the same person for you. An unknown world opened up before you, and you realized that I, too, have come from there. You understood how little you truly know about me. Maybe out of tact, or maybe out of cowardice, but you never grubbed around in the foulnesses that, with benevolent obfuscation, are called *the past*. That I have another, secret life that I never spoke about with you. After five years of marriage, you had to think you barely knew me.

I knew it was over at that moment. Everything I had built up, guarded, and tended for years was over. There was not even an escape route, as I had supposed up till then, nor did I know why I had thought there might be one in the first place.

What was it you wanted to know about me? Everything, you replied. Everything we had kept quiet about until now. Yet you still did not know where to start. With who this Kingbitter actually was, perhaps. He was under the impression that he was Bee's best friend, I replied. Bee didn't have any best friends, however, because he had no time for friendship and had no need of friends. You weren't happy with how familiarly he spoke about me. Why? What did he say? Never mind. It was odd. As if . . .

Yes, I was his lover. To his credit, it has to be said that he found that hard to cope with, deceiving his friend and mentor, his idol. I displayed little understanding of his moral qualms: he was what I needed, him and no one else. I was driven by an obsession of some kind at the time; I wanted to destroy my body because by then Bee, my husband, the one I loved, wasn't so much as touching it.

I remember that morning. When I awoke, Bee, my husband, was no longer beside me; he was obviously in the hall (that's how we referred to the apartment: a single room with hall)—anyway, plainly sitting and writing in the windowless hall. He was always writing or translating or reading. All I saw of him most of the time was his back. I drew the curtain; it was a sunny early-summer morning, with the fragrances of distant flowers managing to waft their way even into the city. A new day had begun, just as superfluously as I myself was standing there superfluously in my nightdress. Not a sound was to be heard, nothing stirred. I felt an urge to cry. Not sniffle, whimper, or blubber, no, but to howl, screaming, slobbering, runny-nosed, hammering the walls with my fists. It suddenly crossed my mind that I couldn't do that at home. The apartment was too small; everything would be overheard. I dressed quickly, that suppressed sobbing choking my throat, and rushed down onto the street. The tears had already started flowing meanwhile, and I was cudgeling my brains to figure out where I could go to have a cry. A coffeehouse or public place was out of the question. At the clinic, my colleague's consulting hours would already be under way. I don't like using public conveniences. I was crossing a broad open square. I remember that there was a raised stretch of curbstones running beside two sets of tramlines to separate the rails from the roadway. For some reason, I carried on along that narrow strip, with cars swishing past my feet. Did I just turn my ankle, or suddenly spot the simplest solution? I didn't fall; only one foot slipped off the paving stones. There was a horrendous screeching of brakes behind me. I looked straight into the driver's eyes through the windscreen. He was probably an occupational driver. He was deathly pale, staring fixedly ahead, his face frozen in an expression of horror, and I abruptly grasped the state into which I had slipped: without asking, I had made another person part of my fate, all but killed him, on a seemingly innocuous summer morning. He drove on without uttering a word, and I continued without uttering a word. I then found myself in a stairway, walked up to the second floor, and rang a doorbell. Luckily, it opened. I literally shoved an astonished Kingbitter to one side, threw myself onto the couch, and, lying flat on my belly, at last began to howl out loud, uninhibitedly, pounding the couch with my fist. Out of the corner of my eye I could see Kingbitter's shadow hovering, mute and motionless. Later he drew closer. He started interrogating me, then eventually made efforts to comfort me. After that we went to bed. Surprised, I surrendered myself with relief to the surging orgasms, which I likewise greeted with wild shrieks—something I never normally do. It was the first time I had been unfaithful to Bee. That too was a solution, albeit not the simplest or the most perfect one.

"Did you love him?"

"I can't really answer that, Adam. No doubt I loved him, and no doubt I hated him as well. That's neither here nor there. Whether it was love or not, we were tied to each other by bonds of a different kind."

"What kind?"

"All kinds. You wouldn't understand any of them."

"Is it true you've met up with him?"

"It's true."

"Several times? Often? Did you sleep with him?"

"No. And what if I had? What difference would that make?"

"True, what difference would that make?" you muttered. There was a flash of hostile rage in your eyes—for the first time since we had known each other. I'm sorry. You said you wanted to know me; well, get to it. But don't expect me to help.

It had grown chillier in the meantime. We went into the living room. I love our living room, Adam. Especially like that, in the evening, in the velvety glow of the clever lighting. I asked you to close the door to the terrace. I felt cold. You can light a fire if you want, you said; it's already laid in the fireplace. Light it, I replied; let it burn. I asked for a drink, a stiff one: cognac. You rummaged in the liquor cabinet. It seemed the cognac had run out. A vodka, then. Finnish or Russian? Russian; only Russian will do. We clinked glasses. You seemed to have been placated.

"That man," you said, "claims there is a manuscript . . . A novel . . ."

"There isn't," I said.

"He maintains there is . . ."

"There was."

"A novel?"

"Let's say. That's what Kingbitter would call it."

"That is indeed how he put it. A novel, he said, that B. finished before his suicide and handed over to you . . ."

"Yes, that's right."

"So it exists after all!"

"No, it doesn't," I said.

"Then where is it?"

"It was burnt."

"Burnt?" you said in amazement. "Where?"

I pointed to the fireplace: "There."

"You burned it?"

"Yes."

You paused a little, waiting for me to say something more. I said nothing. You ought to have seen that I had no wish to offer any explanations. You asked nonetheless why I had burned the novel, or whatever it was. Because he asked me to, I replied. That was not sufficient reason, you said. You cited examples of artists who had instructed heirs that they wished to have any works that were left behind incinerated, but in reality had not wanted that at all.

"He did," I assured you.

"Then why didn't he burn it himself?"

"Because he wanted me to do it."

"And what if you hadn't? What if that was precisely why he entrusted it to you?"

"The reason he entrusted it to me was because he knew for sure that I would do it."

"How could he have known that?"

From it being our secret compact, the consummation, the higher sense, the apotheosis of our relationship. Not that I could tell you that; I had taken you aback quite enough as it was. I reiterated that it had been Bee's last wish. A somewhat lame excuse, I realized.

But why did you need explanations? Why did you push it to breaking point? Why did you pull faces as if you were holding me responsible? Had I had no qualms, you asked with a troubled look, that I was destroying something important, something valuable? That was odd, more than odd, the way you started defending Bee *against me.* I know what was behind it: honor, your hobbyhorse. I could do nothing to help you, Adam, nothing. I had never seen you before as foolish, clueless, ridiculous; I had always seen you in the most favorable situations, indeed always took great care to view you solely in the most favorable situations. I have a thousand memories of you, ten thousand. I always felt your sure, warm hand on my back, my shoulder, my body. You would take me to the hospital at night. We would look in to see how our children were sleeping. I would lie with you in bed, eyes misted from happiness, my head resting on your shoulder. I loved watching you play tennis, loved the way you stood in front of your drawing table, studying an emerging plan with head tipped to one side. I loved you, and it drove me almost to despair to see you backed into such an undeserved corner. I toyed with you like a cat with a mouse, and you have to believe it was not because I wanted it that way but because you entered into a sanctum of my secrets in which I alone know my way around—to the extent that is possible.

Did I at least read it through before . . .

. . . I tossed it onto the fire? I finished the sentence. I did.

What was it like?

How do you mean?

You became flustered.

"I mean . . . was it any good, or bad?"

"What does good or bad mean with a novel? Anyway, he himself never called it a novel."

"What did he call it, then?"

"A 'manuscript,' 'my piece.' "

"What was it about? What was the story?"

I hesitated before plunging in all the same.

"The struggle of a man and woman. They love each other to start with, but later on the woman wants a child from the man, and he is unable to forgive the woman for that. He subjects the woman to various miseries in order to break and undermine her faith in the world. He drives her into a severe psychological crisis, to the verge of suicide, and when he realizes this, he himself commits suicide instead of the woman."

You were silent. Then you asked why the man was punishing the woman merely because she wanted a child.

"Because it is not permissible to want anything."

"Why not?"

"Because of Auschwitz."

Something appeared to dawn on you. Didn't the story somewhat resemble the story of my own marriage with Bee, you asked, at least judging from what you had been able to gather from me? No, I replied, I never wanted to take my own life. You then again asked if I was sure I hadn't misunderstood Bee's intentions. Writers sometimes "cast themselves into the most profound depths of despair," you said, in order to master it and move on.

"Bee, however, committed suicide," I reminded you.

"True," you conceded.

"In any case, Bee never considered himself to be a writer," I said.

That surprised you, I could see.

"But he wrote . . ."

"Because that was his sole means of expression. A person's true means of expression, however, he was always saying, is his life. Living the shame of life and maintaining silence, that was the greatest accomplishment of all. How many times he came out with that, oh, how many times, to the point of insanity."

How had the manuscript gotten into my hands? you wanted to know.

He gave it to me.

Where.

In his apartment.

You didn't lose your head; you exercised great self-control. So it was true that I had paid visits to him, you concluded. No, it's not; but this time he called, and I went. It was the first time I had seen his concrete cell, as he jokingly called it. It was pretty dismal. But then I noticed Sarah's flowers in a vase on the table. I placed my own beside them. I was glad about Sarah's flowers; you're in good hands with Sarah, I told him. He smiled. He took the bundle of paper out of a wardrobe, from beneath the underwear. "Read it through later," he said. "What's this?" "What did you use to call it? An indictment of life." He smiled again. No one in the world had a smile as sad as his. I gingerly turned the conversation to cutting back on the drug intake. He didn't protest: "We'll talk about that later." The next morning he had the farewell letter delivered to me by post. It was all planned in advance, precisely, like the perfect crime.

I held my tongue about that, however—not that you don't have a right to know everything about me. I could see that you too were being driven by some sort of nemesis, Adam, you wanted to get to the bottom of something, and what that was maybe you yourself did not know. We had never spoken about him, or if we did, it was only ever very circumspectly, but now you suddenly wanted to know everything about Bee and about my marriage to him. You were trying, you said, to picture the man. The climate around him; how I had been able to live with him. I asked you not to do it. Why not? Because, I said, it's humiliating. What's humiliating about it? The depths to which a person can sink, I said. What did I mean by that? How deep? Low, right down to the Auschwitz horizon; to the point where a person loses her bearings, her will, abandons her goals, loses herself.

"Yet you still stayed with him."

That was true.

"Why? I'd like to know the reason why!"

Yes, there had been a time when that question tormented me too: Why? I think that extraordinary life mesmerized me. An odd word, but no other one fits: mesmerized. I fell under his spell. It took time, but I gradually recognized where our life was headed. We had begun to exhaust all the possibilities of defying destruction, as I read in a book by a French writer that Bee handed to me. There was something systematic about it. All one had to do was step across a borderline and one would be liberated, as it were. Or feel relieved, at least. There was a time when it was still possible to speak with Bee. We talked about words once—words and neuroses, or word phobias, to be more precise. He recounted his own word phobias, the ones he had been taunted with in childhood and had subsequently made a conscious effort to surmount. He asked me if I had any such phobias. He had a quite extraordinary flair for prying out painful experiences. There was no hiding from his questions. All at once, the dread words of my girlhood days were there: *the Jewish secret.* I had always said that to myself in a deep, bristling tone, closing my eyes as I did so. It was a kind of trigger for the other words about which I was phobic: *Auschwitz. Killed. Destroyed. Perished. Survived.* It brought back everything, my oppressive childhood, spent in the shadow of such words. My mother died of some disease she had brought back from Auschwitz; my father was a *survivor,* a mute, lonely, unapproachable man. I don't know how I still managed to grow up into a more or less healthy woman. Every day I had to struggle for sanity in order to remain normal. I hated being Jewish, and hated denying it even more. I suffered from a regular neurosis, like so many others; and like them, I too saw just one way out, which was to get used to it. Next to Bee, however, I learned that this was not enough. You have to travel the road to the end, he was always saying. My road leads nowhere; don't look where it is going to, but where it started from.

As a result, then, the way to gain liberation slowly dawned within me. Hard as it was, I recognized that Auschwitz was my bridegroom . . . The meeting with Bee had been no mere accident. It was as if I had known that I would someday have to get to the bottom of the riddle of my life, and the only way of doing that was somehow to live Auschwitz. Bee himself lived Auschwitz here, in Budapest, not of course an Auschwitz comparable to Auschwitz itself but a voluntarily accepted, domesticated Auschwitz, though one in which it was just as possible to perish as in the real one. I could not have lived Auschwitz here, in Budapest, with anyone else except Bee. I was undoubtedly not up to what he was capable of: I suffered, whereas he remained cold. His single-mindedness at times drove me to the verge of madness. He was radical, unmerciful, even brutal in his self-destruction. Initially, I thought that it was a pity for his talent. Later on, though, I understood that he applied his whole talent to Auschwitz, that he was a past master and exclusive artist of the Auschwitz mode of existence. He felt that he had been born illegally, had remained alive for no reason, and nothing could justify his existence unless he were to "decipher the code name Auschwitz." You see, he had a book in English, though I have no idea how he came by it. Like him, the author of that book wrote under his prison name: Ka-Tzetnik 135633. In it were a few lines that Bee quoted so many times I know them by heart: "And even those who were there don't know Auschwitz . . . Auschwitz is another planet, while we humankind, occupants of Planet Earth, have no key to decipher the code name Auschwitz." He sought to decipher it nonetheless, staked his life on it. He did not seek to decipher it philosophically, however, nor scientifically, nor even in his writings. He chose a much more dangerous approach, and thereby became much more dangerous for everyone, and for me above all—no, that's unfair, for himself first and foremost. Because he—how can I explain this? He sought to apprehend Auschwitz in his own life, in his own daily life, in the way he lived. He wished to register on himself (*register:* he was fond of that word) the destructive forces, the survival urge, the mechanism of accommodation, in the same way as physicians of the past used to inject themselves with a poison in order to experience its effects for themselves.

One day I realized that I had given up resisting. No, that's not quite right: one day I realized that I was satisfied. I was startled, because there were no grounds for being satisfied. I was obliged to grasp that I had stepped over that certain borderline. I had burnt out. I regretted my young life, but I was unwilling to do anything about it. I had no desire, no goal, I didn't wish to die but I didn't care to live either. It was a peculiar condition but, in its singular way, not unpleasant.

At some point the instinct for life awakened in me. In actual fact, we were living an impossible life. We had few contacts with people, and with those few people we engaged in forlorn, "nonconformist" conversations. We inhabited a land of rabbit breeders and mushroom producers. My medical colleagues, for the most part, gave in. Each of them had a battered car, a so-called country cabin, several children, and a marriage, good or bad. Every three years they would cash in that tourist currency allowance-thingamajig and, those few dollars in pocket, go off on some trip to the West. I despised them. I was proud of my privileged outcast status. One evening, however, among the *Shivitti* books, books by Katzenelson, Jean Améry, and Borowski, I spotted a gaudy picture album on Bee's desk. It contained a number of the major pieces in the Uffizi gallery, beautifully reproduced on large folios. Also lying there was a ragged yellow-covered volume of Valéry's essay on Leonardo. He needed these for a translation he was doing. That evening he talked about Leonardo and Michelangelo. It is impossible to place them in the human world, he said. Impossible to understand how their work survived, he said. It is impossible to comprehend how anything that attests to greatness has survived; it is obviously a result of innumerable chance events and of human incomprehension, he said. If people had understood the greatness of those works, they would have destroyed them long ago. Fortunately, people have lost their flair for greatness and only their flair for murder has persisted, though undoubtedly they have refined the latter, their flair for murder, to an art, almost to the point of greatness, he said. As a matter of fact, he said, if one examines the contemporary arts more closely, one discovers that a single branch of art has been developed to perfection, and that is the art of murder. He continued along those lines until I broke down, until in the end I was engulfed by what was now an almost familiar wave of indifference.

I don't know what happened to me the next day. I remember the weather was truly splendid, sunlight sparkling on windows, on metal and glass surfaces. People were seated at sun-drenched tables in front of a number of cafés. I had the feeling that the world around me was bubbling with gaiety. I had nothing in my head. I simply went into a so-called bank branch and arranged what had to be arranged, then into a travel agency. I booked two places on a conducted tour to Florence. That day Bee was more relentless than ever. He did not understand my decision, he said. Did I have no sense of the preposterousness of this decision, this act, this affront? He did not understand how I could have imagined that he would get up from his desk and go to Florence in the company of a bunch of numbskulls. He did not understand what business he would have with Florence. He did not understand how I could possibly have imagined him in Florence. He did not understand how I could imagine Florence, imagine that such an entity as "Florence" could exist at all for him. And if this alleged Florence did indeed exist, then it did not exist for him, Bee. Indeed, Florence did not exist even for the Florentines, because the Florentines had clearly, long, long ago, lost sight of what Florence signified. Florence signified nothing to the Florentines, just as it signified nothing to him either. He did not understand my huge, unpardonable blunder of acting as if the world was not a world of murderers, and of wishing to settle myself snugly down in it. He did not understand how I imagined Florence was not a Florence of murderers when everything nowadays belongs to murderers. And so on, on and on. But before he had managed to drive me into total despair, I asked him point-blank whether he wanted to come to Florence or not. He was utterly stunned. What had he been saying all along? he asked. In other words, no, I said. In other words, no, he said. Then I'll go alone, I said. He took that in, but I could see he was startled. In the days that followed, I noticed him more than once making a hesitant motion, as if there were something more that he wished to say. But then he would say nothing. In truth, we exchanged barely more than a few words, and those always the most impersonal, absolutely necessary words. After which I packed my bags and set off on the trip. I myself couldn't say why. I was not at all in the mood. I was impelled by sheer obstinacy, nothing else.

It was on that trip that I met you, Adam. You told me later that I drove you to veritable distraction, because it seemed to you that I was taking no notice of you. Of course I noticed you. I could see you were interested in me. On one occasion you found some pretext to come up to me in the hotel lobby. Another time you courteously offered a helping hand on the steep steps of the excursion bus. You passed some witty remark about one of the paintings. I made up my mind that if you were to speak to me just once more I would say straight out, Don't bother, my dear tennis champ (there was something about you that indicated you liked playing tennis), don't make an effort, this one's not for bedding. Not because you don't attract me, but I'm sorry to say I have no libido. I'm frigid, as they say.

All the same, your letter moved me. I had not received a love letter since I was a teenager, and then only once. With great discretion, you addressed it to the clinic. The empathy of the opening lines touched me: you had never in your life seen such an unhappy woman's face, you wrote. So unhappy did I look that—I should excuse the frankness—the effect was erotic. You were increasingly fantasizing about my face, you wrote, "that pallid, exciting face." What if you were to manage to coax some expression into it, an unexpected gleam of interest? The first smile. "And I try to picture what this face must be like in moments of ecstasy . . ." —you see, I recall your every word. I stuffed it away in my drawer, among the jumble of prescription pads, business cards, and other bits of paper.

I didn't take you seriously. How could I? After all, what chance were you able to offer me? I no longer saw any need for a lover, still less for a good friend. After my return home from Florence, Bee and I were barely on speaking terms. Strange as it may seem, though, that in itself was no impetus to make changes to my life. After all, and I never lost sight of this, I couldn't fault Bee; when all was said and done, I had not hooked up with him for a happily married life. So natural did my life feel, my state of being lost along with Bee, that it made me all but arrogant. So natural was it for me to be consumed, destroyed, annihilated in my marriage that the very possibility of choice did not pass through my head. Of what interest to me were unproblematic existences, straightforward success stories, orderly circumstances, sporting lives, love of one's profession! I held you in deep disdain, I must confess.

I don't know when I noticed that something had changed in me. Most likely your persistence did it. You would pop up time and time again; you called me up, waited for me in the street in front of the clinic. My attempts to avoid you, to make myself repudiate you, were useless: you would always be there again, always with the same reassuring expression, the same slightly apologetic smile. The only thing that changed each time was your necktie. Nonetheless, one evening, I sat down with you in a café. Then, one morning, I was surprised to catch myself standing before a shopwindow and looking at neckties.

Suddenly, words tumbled out of me unprepared. It was one evening, getting back home at some late hour from your place. Bee was still seated at his desk, writing or reading, reading or writing, reading *and* writing—it's all the same. I asked if he was at all interested where I had been every evening recently. He did not reply. I then expressed my thanks to him in my own way. I no longer remember what words I used. I expressed my thanks that through him I had come to understand everything that I had not understood, had not even dared to understand, by reason of my parents, my family, my entire monstrous heritage. I understood everything now, and now I was ready for my response. You are probably right, Bee, that the world is a world of murderers, I told him, but all the same I don't wish to see the world as a world of murderers; I wish to see the world as a place in which it is possible to live. He accepted that. He let me go. Yet it was still as though there were some issue, and a very vital issue at that, left unresolved between the two of us. I would have been unable to formulate what that murky point was, but neither of us had a clear conscience. It was as if we both felt that we still owed each other something.

Next to you, however, I calmed down. I learned to forget. I also learned to live together—not just with you but also with myself. You may still remember what my response to you was that evening when you asked how I had found the strength to burn the manuscript.

"You'll be amazed to hear, Adam, that it was you who gave me the strength. You and the children."

So it was. It's a pity you gave up on our compact, Adam. A pity you gave up on our happiness.

There is something else that I must say, though I would rather have kept quiet about it. You may remember that I went away to a dermatology conference in Cracow. Bee's manuscript was in my hands by then, but I had not yet carried out his instruction. I reckoned that I ought to see Auschwitz before doing so. The conference, above all its timing, struck me as being almost propitious. As you probably know, a regular bus service has been established between Cracow and Auschwitz for tourists who are interested. Although I had wanted to make the trip alone, a female colleague caught me just as I was booking the bus ticket at the hotel reception desk. I was therefore unable to avoid being joined by her and, through her, others as well. I was annoyed but supposed I would surely be able to shake them off somehow on getting there. Their chatter in the coach was hard to bear. Finally, however, we pulled up somewhere and entered a forecourt that reminded me of the ticket halls in the bigger bathing places. There were leaflets lying everywhere, in all the world's languages, information on group discounts, and so on. Through the glass screen at the rear of the hall, as a come-on, so to say, you could see the gray stone barracks blocks. People were surging along the narrow paths, men, women, children. The sun was glowing dully behind a mackerel sky. We bought tickets. A presentiment of something gone wrong began to take hold. Everything that I was already well acquainted with from photographs was there. The inscription over the gate, the barbed-wire fences stretched between the recurved concrete posts, the single-story stone buildings—everything with an air of implausibility, like a copy of an original as it were. I found myself unable to capture the right mood, despite having prepared for it for days. I was haunted by a sense of walking around an outdoor folk museum. I was struck by the mischievous notion that an extra dressed in striped prison clothes might pop up at any moment. I saw the piled-up shoes, the suitcases, the heaps of hair, all displayed with the meticulousness of museum exhibits, without managing to achieve any close relation with them, to regard them as my own shoes, my own suitcase, my own hair. The people gawking behind my back occasionally shoved me; at other times, one or another of my colleagues who perpetually kept turning up said something to me. Someone asked if it was permitted to light a cigarette. Tears were streaming down the face of an elderly woman. The general hum of conversation never let up for a single moment. A colleague next to me remarked, "You have to go to Birkenau, that's the real McCoy." "What's 'Birkenau'?" another asked. I tried to detach myself from our group, but they always caught up with me. Someone warned me not to miss the bus that would be leaving to go back. I can't return like this, I thought to myself, without having accomplished anything. It was the sort of notion that sometimes haunts one in dreams, when one can hear the words but does not understand them. What indeed was it that I ought to *accomplish?* I didn't know. It was a mistake for me to come here, I thought, all a mistake. When we got back to the hotel, one of our colleagues discovered to her horror that her purse had vanished. The receptionist enlightened her that Auschwitz was teeming with pickpockets, who took advantage of the visitors' deeply emotional state and attendant inattentiveness. That night I couldn't sleep and was overcome by occasional fits of sobbing.

YOU HAD ALL GONE—TO THE OFFICE OR NURSERY school. I called in sick to the clinic. I lit the fire, brought the manuscript down from my room, then sat down on the carpet in front of the fire. First the manuscript, page by page, finally the farewell letter.

> *Without any ulterior motive or pathos, without the slightest intention of emotional blackmail, I ask, indeed demand, that you destroy this manuscript as a private letter from the hereafter that no one has written and that is addressed to no one. My wish is no sudden whim; I have had time to think it through carefully, so consider it final and irrevocable. Throw it onto a fire so it burns, because via the flames it will reach where it has to reach . . .*

Not for one second did I feel that I was alone. It was as if we were gazing at the fire together.

> *My imagination was inadequate, my means were inadequate, and it is no consolation that others too have failed to find the means . . . I do at least know, however, that one's sole means is, at one and the same time, one's sole possession: one's life.*

I understood; I grasped every word.

> *You must incinerate the document in which I place our pitiful and fleeting story in your hands—you, in whom, innocently and without your being acquainted with Auschwitz, Auschwitz scored the deepest wound.*

Yes, I had to accept what he intended for me; this life dedicated to Auschwitz could not burn out without a trace.

The writing flared up, over and over again, amid the flames.

. . . by virtue of the authority I have lived through and suffered for you, and for you alone, I revoke Auschwitz . . .

Anyone who stays alive is always guilty. But I shall bear the wound.

(The sitting room of Adam and Judit's villa. The lights are still on, even though dawn is already breaking behind the picture windows. The glass door that opens onto the garden is closed. Dying embers in the fire grate.

Adam and Judit—weary, having obviously spent a sleepless night.

Prolonged silence.

Judit now gets to her feet and silently starts gathering ashtrays and glasses.)

ADAM: There is another way of telling the story, Judit.

JUDIT *(pauses)*: How?

ADAM: The way it happened.

JUDIT: Do you think I'm lying?

ADAM: I'm sure you're not. I have listened to you closely. I can recall practically every word you said. You told an Auschwitz-tinged love story, Judit.

JUDIT *(astounded)*: Auschwitz-tinged! . . . What's that supposed to mean? What can *you* know about Auschwitz?

ADAM: Everything that it is possible to read. Though, for all that, I know nothing about it. Just as you can know nothing about it either.

JUDIT: It's not the same thing. I'm Jewish.

ADAM: That in itself means nothing. Everyone is Jewish.

JUDIT: You amaze me, Adam. You have a philosopher's wit. I would never have imagined it of you . . . For instance, that you read about Auschwitz.

ADAM: Ever since I got to know you, Judit, incessantly. One book after another. You will find a whole library of Auschwitz literature in my office. Inexhaustible.

JUDIT: You never said a word to me.

ADAM: No, because I could see you were fleeing. Only I was not to know that you were really fleeing from your love. You lived with me, but in your dreams you were being unfaithful with him.

JUDIT: So that's what this is about. You're jealous of a dead man.

ADAM: That may be. But there was no other way of understanding you, what impelled the two of you. Him to write his penitent opus, which he then goes on to condemn to death, along with himself; and you to carry out the sentence and thereby partake in the experience of some kind of mystic union, if I understand what you said.

JUDIT: And you understand now, perhaps?

ADAM: I've read at least fifteen books about manic depression and paranoia.

(Long silence.)

ADAM: No one can revoke Auschwitz, Judit. No one, and by virtue of no authority. Auschwitz is irrevocable.

JUDIT *(in growing distress)*: I was there. I saw. Auschwitz does not exist.

ADAM *(steps to Judit and grabs her roughly by the shoulders)*: I have two children, two half-Jewish children. They know nothing as yet. They are asleep. Who is going to tell them about Auschwitz? Which of us is going to tell them they are Jewish?

(Prolonged silence. Adam tightly grips Judit's shoulders.)

JUDIT *(quietly, almost plaintively)*: And what if we were not to tell them? . . .

CURTAIN

In the bundle of handwritten notes, however, Kingbitter had also come across another, certainly more radical, ending, although its free-verse form pointed to an earlier date of conception, and thus it would have been more a prototype than a genuine alternative to the final version of the text.

ADAM:

He killed the child in you
You killed his book

You incinerated it in fire just as at Auschwitz
Worthy revenge perhaps subconscious as they say
I won't dwell on which of you is a killer
but it's a dreadful insight
I'm only just starting to see See and understand
I understand the anger
understand the horror
understand the concealment
understand what it means
to be Jewish
I understand the judgment
I understand it

JUDIT:
You were innocent and strong
Now it's all at an end
I knew it would come to this
that he would come after me
trample me in the mud
pulverize me
I knew there was no escape

ADAM:
I have two children
Two half-Jewish children
Who's going to tell them the story of Auschwitz
Who's going to tell them they're Jewish

JUDIT:
All I admired in you is over
You've turned weak hysterical cowardly and witty

ADAM:
Let it not be a Jew they learn it from

I shall tell them in good time
Let them not learn dread

JUDIT:

But you are already dreading it yourself
How familiar this is to me Adam
How much I did not want this
This was my life with Bee
At times he was dismayed lost his head
It's shameful to live he screamed tugging his hair
Shameful to live Shameful to live
I screamed too I love you Bee
I screamed Calm down now
Shameful to live Shameful to live
Love me I pleaded . . .
(She suddenly falls silent.
A brief pause.)

ADAM:

You mean . . . love?

JUDIT:

That's our only chance.

ADAM:

Love! *(He suddenly laughs out loud.)*

JUDIT:

Love! *(She, too, is infected by hysterical laughter.)*
(Adam snatches some light object off the table—his cigarette pack, say—and tosses it toward Judit. Judit likewise snatches something—a cushion, say—and aims it at Adam. Out of this an impromptu, ruthless, precarious juggling game develops between them: while they fixate on the word, furnishing it with the most

diverse emphases and emotional nuances, playing ball with it so to speak, objects that they pick up from the table, the chairs, this place and that, and fling at each other fly through the air.)

BOTH TOGETHER:

Love! Love? Love . . . Love.

(Words whirl around, objects whirl around.)

CURTAIN

Kingbitter lifted the reading glasses from his nose and gazed impassively at the sickening dance tripped by the motes of dust and dirt drifting about in the room like malignant microbes in the shafts of afternoon sunlight blazing in through the window. As on every occasion that he took the play out, the feeling Kingbitter was left with as he came to the end was again one of having been cheated and deprived. Among the handwritten notes there was a reminder, the sort of practical advice that writers and authors often record for themselves, in writing or on tape, to ensure they don't lose sight of what they are actually writing. Kingbitter did not open the reminder on the screen before him, but he had already seen it so many times that he knew it off by heart. "The play's raison d'être," the note ran, "is a novel. Its reality is thus another work. On top of that, we have no knowledge of this other work, the novel, in its entirety, any more than we do of the Creation. It is thus just as baffling as the world that is given to us, which we refer to under its alternative name of reality. Just as fragmentary, yet just as intelligible, for after all, we live in accordance with the logic of the world that is given to us."

Except that the reality granted to Kingbitter, as a result of the arbitrariness of the given plot, had simply vanished from Kingbitter's purview, and he was now gazing after it in the same way he was gazing at the faraway, random movements of the motes of dust, which resembled some kind of extrasensory sign language—compelling yet incomprehensible. As on every occasion that he got to the end of the play, Kingbitter posed to himself the Hamlet question, which for him did not run "To be or not to be," but "Am I or am I not"? But then his world was a world of manuscripts, he had always spent his life among manuscripts, revolved around manuscripts; one might go so far as to say that his path in life was flanked on all sides by manuscripts, so it was not entirely illogical that he should, in the end, perceive the stumbling block of his fate to be a manuscript—an incinerated manuscript.

Kingbitter laughed, and now too this abrupt noise sounded more like a sharp snort than a laugh. *Finita la commedia,* he thought, perhaps unclear himself whether he meant the play or was thinking of another, possibly broader frame of reference—life, or even reality, so-called reality, that is to say. Maybe it had been a pity to read through the play; on the other hand, he had gotten into the habit of reading it through from time to time. For whatever reason, it somehow reminded him of more splendid times—at least it seemed to him now that they had been more splendid times. Indubitably, Kingbitter had once, long ago, had convictions; indeed, it would be fair to say that his convictions had guided his life. As he happened right then to be standing at the window again and watching the down-and-outs, it occurred to him that once, long ago, he had also watched the down-and-outs with different eyes. Once, long ago, in his intellectual arrogance, Kingbitter had made a claim to feeling sorry for those people; he had pulled a thick, sticky wall of sympathy between the down-and-outs and himself in order to flaunt his own social sensibility. He had taken an active part in movements that made use of the down-and-outs to hold up their very existence as an outrage that flew in the face of a dictatorship whose justification for its very existence was grounded in social equity.

Nowadays the down-and-outs were no longer of any interest to Kingbitter. That may have been what drew him so irresistibly to them. On the one hand, he felt a twinge of guilt, as if he had, in some sense, left them in the lurch. On the other hand, Kingbitter could not deny it, their games and ceremonies were a source of diversion for him. The way they arrived. The way they greeted a newcomer. The bags. The objects that they produced from them. The greasy fingers that carved the hunks of bacon fat on sheets of newspaper they laid out on the benches. The enormous jackknives. The flasks. The faces, the clothes, the costumes (so to say). Their laughter.

Kingbitter was sometimes given to reflect that while venom and fury were often to be seen on those faces, he almost never saw grief or melancholy. He had slowly come to recognize that these people had no reason to be melancholy, as they had no memories, having lost them or settled their accounts with them, and so in actual fact had no past—nor any future, it's true. They lived in a state of the continuous present, in which bare existence showed itself as both an immediate and exclusive reality, whether in varying forms of worry and privation or the fleeting delights of escapism. They were *storyless people,* and that notion awakened a tacit sympathy in Kingbitter. He was well aware, of course, that each of them had their own sad story that had brought them to this, but Kingbitter supposed that by the time they had been brought to this, those stories had long lost any significance (if such stories can have any significance at all).

Since being liberated from his superfluous complexes, Kingbitter had indubitably thought about the down-and-outs more easily, one might say more humanely. Besides which, he had never been able to eliminate the possibility that, one fine day, he might find himself there on the bench. Not today, it ran through his mind, and not tomorrow, but maybe the day after tomorrow. Why not? Kingbitter was unacquainted with any law or any human being able or willing to preserve him from that.

This by-no-means gratifying thought did not run through Kingbitter's mind unprompted. He recalled that this morning he had originally wanted, so to say, "to work"; there were even two manuscripts lying on his desk, awaiting his editorial attention. But even as he was correcting the first few pages, he had been overcome by a leaden dispiritedness. Sooner or later, Kingbitter would be obliged to acknowledge that he had tired of his line of business. Simply become bored of judging whether a book was good or bad, because nowadays that question had become a matter of complete indifference to Kingbitter, even though he made his living from the decisions he made on such questions, that was his occupation; and if he were to continue being indifferent to these questions, then he would have neither livelihood nor occupation. His ex-wife had probably been right when, in the course of a conversation years before, she had advised Kingbitter to change jobs. "You don't understand the voice of the times," his ex-wife had told him, and Kingbitter had agreed with her, haughtily and contemptuously, because his wife was always right, and that was why Kingbitter had always treated her with disdain.

Dusk was drawing in. Gloom was beginning to settle on his room, to which Kingbitter, standing at the window, had his back turned. Only the spectral glow of the computer screen glimmered from the dim corner of the room; Kingbitter had forgotten to switch it off, it seems. He had launched an operation on it that he might have forgotten about, or left incomplete, and the machine was now urgently flashing toward Kingbitter's back, in its own insufferably stubborn way, its futile interrogatives:

Next step
Cancel